The villagers of Stoney Cross are preparing for their
"Gr   estival,
and   ter to
adve   n extra
friss   rns to
dism 19 FEB 2020   ughby,
mov   ore the
festi   wledge
of pe   d never
to se   n he is
foun   to this
welt   lconer,
his   Davey"
Car   andit"
cou

CHOKED OFF

ANDREA FRAZER

LARGE
PRINT

First published in Great Britain 2013
by
Accent Press

First Isis Edition
published 2019
by arrangement with
Accent Press

A catalogue record for this book is available
from the British Library.

ISBN 978–1–78541–642–2 (hb)
ISBN 978–1–78541–648–4 (pb)

DRAMATIS PERSONAE

<u>The Residents of Stoney Cross:</u>
Culverwell, Lydia — amateur pianist
Horsfall-Ertz, Harriet "Squirrel" — dog-lover
and hoarder
Jephcott, Delia — flautist living with Ashley Rushton
Leighton, Summer — young dancer
Lyddiard, Serena — working in the health service
Markland, Camilla — harpist, married to Gregory
McKnight, Peregrine — joint tenant of The Inn
on the Green
Palister, Sadie — sculptress
Pargeter, Fiona — amateur singer, married to Rollo
Radcliffe, Tarquin — joint tenant of The Inn
on the Green
Ravenscastle, Rev. Benedict — vicar, married to Adella
Rushton, Ashley — living with Delia Jephcott
Templeton, Christobel — amateur poet, married to
Jeremy, romantic novelist
Westinghall, Felicity — romantic novelist, married to
Hugo, also a writer
Willoughby, Marcus — radio presenter who is new in
the village
Wingfield-Heyes, Araminta "Minty" — painter

Sundry Exhibiting Artists:
Carstairs, Emelia — pastels
Fitch, Lionel — oils
Solomons, Rachel — watercolours

Officials:

Detective Inspector Harry Falconer
Acting Detective Sergeant Ralph "Davey" Carmichael
Sergeant Bob Bryant
PC Merv Green
WPC Linda "Twinkle" Starr
Superintendent Derek "Jelly" Chivers
Dr Philip Christmas

FOREWORD

A Few Notes on Stoney Cross — Then and Now

The village of Stoney Cross is situated some four miles from Castle Farthing and nine miles from the town of Carsfold. Five miles in the other direction is Market Darley.

Just over a hundred years ago Stoney Cross had been a perfect centre for the community that had lived in its environs. It had its own school, church and chapel. The forge, with its blacksmith and farrier, attended to the needs of the farmers' one-horsepower four-footed engines, the High Street for the demands of their wives and households. It had a mill for flour and a flat field for recreation on its outskirts. At Starlings' Nest, a local doctor held surgery twice a week for the inhabitants' physical problems, and the reverend gentleman at The Rectory took care of their spiritual needs.

The village, then known as Stoney Acre, this being before the Great War (the 1914 to 1918 one, not the Napoleonic, also referred to as the Great War of its time), was a small but busy commercial centre, its highways and byways frequented by horses, carts and carriages. For two hundred years its inn had been a staging-house for coaches, and on its side were stables for the tired horses, above its bars, rooms for the weary travellers.

It had been renamed Stoney Cross in 1925 when the war memorial was erected, declaring the deaths of so many young male members of its community. About this time, with the decline of the horse, so many fewer men left to work the land and the introduction of machinery, farming changed for ever. The strong, lusty young men who once worked the fields had left a hole that it was impossible to fill, and the machines moved in to take their places, leading to the inevitable decline, and finally closure, of the forge — there was not much money to be made from decorative ironwork. The farrier, too, walked away from his previously busy life in Stoney Cross, never to return.

Over the next few decades, the fortunes of Stoney Cross fell into decline. People moved away, as small businesses closed due to financial problems, or the lack of an heir to carry on with the business. Many buildings and houses stood empty, as if time had closed over them, encapsulating them in a bubble of the past.

The school closed down due to lack of pupils, the mill following suit, due to lack of businesses to supply, for it was not just Stoney Cross that struggled in this era. Over time, some of the farm buildings were sold off, as was the land, for new housing after the Second World War, and the chapel ceased to hold services, there being no faithful left to listen to the fire and brimstone sermons preached within its walls.

The only things left unchanged were the village green and pond, and the standing stones to the south-west of the village.

Weekenders started its revival first, buying the

smaller outlying properties, then commuters began to move into the more substantial homes, hoping to give their families a healthy life away from the bustle and pollution of more urban areas. Gradually properties were renovated and converted, and Stoney Cross now boasted an old mill conversion, an old school conversion, an old forge conversion, and a refurbished old rectory. The old coaching inn had shaken off its dust and cobwebs, and re-invented itself as The Inn on the Green, with an adjoining restaurant, in actuality the old stables (converted, of course).

The High Street now housed an arts, crafts and new-age centre, a post office (hanging on by the skin of its teeth), a gallery-cum antiques and curios shop, a tea shop, a village store packed with organic-this and organic-that, and, what seemed an amazing survival but was in fact a new arrival, a hardware and corn-merchant's. Down Castle Farthing Road, a Chinese chippie and pizzeria (eat in or take out — home deliveries within a two mile radius) nestled none too shyly, its light blazing from under a bushel, like a beacon to those of less formal dining habits.

The old, flat recreation field was now a football/rugby/cricket pitch with pavilion, and the old village hall, sadly neglected and inadequate, had been replaced with a much larger and grander structure, with the combined functions of Village Hall, Scout/Guide Hut and Sunday school. The village green was home to three benches: a very old one commemorating Queen Victoria's golden jubilee, one to commemorate the coronation of our current Queen, the third in memory of Princess Diana.

On the public open space opposite The Inn on the Green were two "Silver Jubilee" benches, and one of the standing stones had received a brass plaque declaring the start of a new millennium.

This is Stoney Cross today. It even has signs on all roads entering it reading, "Slow — free-range children".

(Author's note: anything in square brackets [] are the author's own comments.)

Prologue

As our story opens, Akela, Brown Owl, and the Sunday school teacher are gathered in the village teashop, casting aspersions on all those involved with the accursed Forthcoming Event. They had been cast out of their normal space for their weekly activities, and were sorely tried, and indignant that this should be allowed to happen.

In The Old Chapel (converted), Christobel Templeton sat at her Georgian desk, putting the finishing touches to her fiercely calligraphic poetry exhibits. She would, of course, not use these for her recitations, as they would be on display. She was a tiny woman with a mass of auburn-tinged curls, freckles, and big brown eyes, and was at present shooing her cats, Byron and Longfellow, away from the un-dried ink. As she resumed her lettering, her small pink tongue protruded, almost invisibly, from the side of her mouth as she concentrated. She so hoped that everyone would like her little contributions, and looked forward, with an anxious, desperate longing, to receiving praise for her efforts.

Across the intervening paddock, at The Old School (also converted), Sadie Palister stood stock still, chisel in one hand, mallet in the other, her head tilted slightly sideways as she viewed her creation with a critical eye from behind her horn-rimmed glasses, her view slightly obscured by the wispy fronds of a raven-black fringe. "This thing *will* be finished in time," she shouted across her studio to no one in particular, flinging down her tools and tossing a cascade of hair away from her face.

She stooped to grab an open can of lager from the floor, and pondered anew how to arrange her other, smaller pieces around this monster, for the great event. Smiling wickedly, she took a greedy gulp of the lukewarm flat liquid, and wandered over to her favourite piece, beside which her contact lenses were sitting. These were of a starting blue, and not only helped her eyesight, but transformed her eyes' natural nondescript colour into tropical pools and, on the whole, she thought, they enhanced her image as a sculptress.

Oh yes, *that* must be blatantly in view, considering its title, and considering also who might see it and tie it in to its inspiration, she thought. (This was a thin hope, as she had no doubt that her old enemy would have little time for such small-fry as a village event, but it cheered her to think that this was, at least, a vague possibility — cheered, but chilled her at the same time!) Her gothic make-up crinkled with mischief, as she ran her pitch-coloured fingernails through her night-black hair.

Across the High Street in The Old Mill (converted, unsurprisingly), Araminta Wingfield-Heyes — Minty to her friends — bent her small, round figure to the bottom right-hand corner of the large canvas before her, her cropped mousey hair almost touching the not quite dry paint. Better sign it, I suppose, she thought, reaching over to her workstation where her brush rested, in waiting for just this moment.

In Dragon Lane, at Journey's End, Lydia Culverwell ran her nimble fingers over the keyboard of her piano in rehearsal for the recitals she would give in the forthcoming event. She had chosen Chopin for her pieces, their sad and romantic themes close to her heart, but at odds with her plain and unremarkable looks. She had had her dull mousey-blonde hair high-lighted in anticipation of, maybe, a photograph in the local newspaper, but could do nothing to disguise the undistinguished grey/blue of her eyes — others in the village, not so naïve, guarded their secret solution to this problem jealously.

As she approached a very tricky section, her ears discerned the unmistakeable "ah-ah-ahing" of her neighbour on the other side of the adjoining wall, obviously warming up with scales, for her own performance. As the intrusive voice searched for a high note it could not quite find, and clung hopelessly to one a quarter of a note lower, Lydia flung down the lid of her "darling" (her pistachio green baby grand), and flounced off to the kitchen to make herself a cup of camomile tea.

She'd wait for now, until the children of the neighbouring household went to bed, then give them hell with the louder sections of Dave Brubeck's "Blue Rondo a la Turk". That would teach the bitch to interrupt her when she was "in the zone".

3

On the other side of the wall, in The (converted) Haven, Fiona Pargeter's cat-like green eyes twinkled with victory and, with a shake of her copper-coloured waves, she launched into her proposed solo for her performance. That had shown the bitch next door that she wasn't the only one around here with a musical bone in her body. As her voice soared higher and higher, she thanked God that her husband Rollo was a sufficiently accomplished pianist to accompany her — how she would have hated to go round on her knees to beg for Lydia's services.

Casting this unpleasant scenario from her thoughts, she let her mind dwell fondly on the fact that Rollo had taken their children George, Henry and Daisy into the village to feed the ducks on the pond. They would not return until tea-time, giving her the rare luxury of peace and quiet, now she had seen off the crashing, mistake-ridden chords of that pretentious cow next door, who would be better off, in her opinion, thumping out melodies for the drunks in The Inn on the Green on a Saturday night.

Down Stoney Stile Lane, in Starlings' Nest, the slightly dumpy figure of Delia Jephcott could be discerned, producing a bright tune on her flute, as beautiful and liquid as birdsong. She had no neighbourhood axe to grind and played on blithely, oblivious to the semi-detached rivalry and warfare underway in Dragon Lane. Oh, but she was hungry! But she mustn't eat anything. No food! Let music be her only sustenance.

Stopping abruptly and putting down her flute, she darted guiltily into the kitchen and opened the fridge. A girl had to eat, hadn't she? And it wasn't as if she couldn't do something about it afterwards, was it? She just mustn't make a habit of it, or she'd have a real problem.

Across the dividing hedge, in Blackbird Cottage, Serena Lyddiard had her earphones in, and was totally absorbed in her graceful dance routine, floating and flying elegantly across the floor of her living room, oblivious to the existence of an outside world, totally caught up in the marriage of music and movement. Her steps suddenly halted, and she pulled her ear-pieces away as she said, "Blast your eyes Tar Baby! What do you think you're doing?" Her eyes smiled fondly at the big black cat, who had unwittingly offered himself as a Fred Astaire to her Ginger Rodgers, and she shooed him off to go play with Ruby, his red-point Siamese companion.

On the other side of Church Lane, opposite the church, in Blacksmith's Cottage, Camilla Markland drew one long, last, lingering chord from her harp and sighed. Her own playing always made her feel emotional. A slightly overweight woman who was constantly on a diet, she was a suicide blonde, dyed by her own hand. She had mud-coloured eyes and, like Sadie Palister, she overcame this shortcoming with the use of turquoise-tinted contact lenses. The sculptress's little secret was only kept, as long as Camilla's was safe in Sadie's bosom. If she, Sadie, ever indicated what she knew, then Stoney Cross would be made aware that

5

Camilla Markland wasn't the only one in the village who was pulling more than wool over her own eyes.

In many other dwellings in Stoney Cross, a welter of individuals were painting, mounting or framing their watercolours, oils and pastels. Portraits, landscapes, and a whole variety of other scenes, were all being treated with the respect due to them, as objects that would soon be on public view, and under the scrutiny of the public's eye.

In other houses, voices were raised oratorically, practising the recitation of poems, short stories, and excerpts from longer literary creations. All much-loved by their creators, these pieces were being treated like new-born babies, each "parent" hoping that their "offspring" would be praised for their beauty, but with the not unnatural dread that they may be slighted as not pretty enough; that they would be mocked, even, for their lack of perfection.

Stoney Cross had become a hub for those of an artistic and creative bent, and was now polishing up its talents for the biggest show the village had produced in living memory.

In the town of Carsfold, Marcus Willoughby was packing up his possessions in preparation for moving to his new home. He had everything "in the bag" workwise between now and Friday, when he would take up residence in his recently purchased dwelling, and thought his new job was going very well indeed. Smiling smugly, he inserted the last few books into a box, and sealed it with parcel tape.

CHAPTER
ONE

Tuesday, 1st September

I

The posters had been up for a month, taped in windows, glued to village noticeboards and pinned to the walls of the public house. They had been pasted on telegraph poles and fences, in fact anywhere that the glaring of the fluorescent yellow background would attract attention. The event had been four months in the planning, from the first nebulous idea, the first vague hope that it really could happen, through all the meetings and arguments, to today.

Today the inhabitants of Stoney Cross began to put into motion their fabulous and exciting plan, the results of which would dazzle those from the surrounding villages and visitors alike. It would be a showcase for the multi-faceted artistic talent of the village's inhabitants, and they waited in great anticipation for what would be "The Stoney Cross Arts Festival" — with luck the first of many over the years to come. This was to take place over the weekend of Saturday the fifth and Sunday the sixth of September, with platforms and exhibition space to show off various artistic gifts harboured within this small community.

There was to be an "Artists Trail" round the homes of those participating, so that their works could be seen in situ: sculptures too heavy to move, watercolours, abstracts; all the categories one could imagine for the visual representations of art, within the limitations, of course, of such a small place.

In the multi-purpose village hall there were to be musical recitals, poetry reading, excerpts from literary works, and a dancing display. The Inn on the Green and the teashop were girding their loins for this onslaught, while at the same time rubbing their hands with glee at the thought of such unexpected profits at the tail-end of the season. (The Festival committee had a strong aversion to the idea of scores of tiny feet thundering and trampling amidst their pretty, ordered village, and also feared for the exhibits, at risk of damage from sticky little fingers and the like, and had decided to stage the event when the schools had reconvened for the new academic year.)

Front gardens had been mown, flower beds weeded, hanging baskets refreshed, and brass door furniture cleaned and polished until it smote the eye with its twinkling glitter. Stoney Cross was on parade, and would not compromise its reputation for being picturesque. The village's collective consciousness shrugged off the word "twee" like an unwanted hand on the shoulder, and concentrated, instead, on the idea of "the perfect place to live", visualising it as envied by others who passed through, or who lived in the surrounding communities, wishing they could live there too.

In the village hall itself, were the several inhabitants who had formed the Festival's committee during its planning stage, plus Hugo Westinghall, a romantic novelist like his wife, and in attendance by invitation. Their two children played under public supervision on the village green, along with their black Labrador, Diabolo. Those gathered were giving the finishing touches to the "lick of paint" to the walls that was deemed necessary for the presentation to the public of the jewels in the local artists' crowns.

Hugo was a small man, only about five feet six inches in height and, as the area he was working on rose higher and higher, he began to make little jumping movements to achieve his goal, leaving small spots of paint on the bald patch revealed by his fast-disappearing mousey hair.

"Get a chair like me, you silly," called his wife Felicity, only five-feet-one herself, and in the process of graduating from a chair to a stepladder. They were both looking forward to the readings from their respective novels, and Felicity had re-hennaed her wispy hair in preparation for looking her best for her public.

"Has anyone had any thoughts on additional publicity?" called Sadie Palister from the other end of the hall where she was crouched, painting almost at floor level. "And I have no idea why I've been involved in this face-lift, as I shall be holding "open house". You know my stuffs much too difficult and expensive to move without a buyer footing the bill." Some of Sadie's sculptures, especially the outdoor ones, literally weighed a ton.

"Serves you right for being on the committee," shouted Hugo Westinghall from his new height on a chair. "I haven't even had that pleasure, and here I am, paintbrush in hand, giving my all for your art."

"Shut up, Hugo!" This was from Sadie.

"What about the local radio station?" Fiona Pargeter, the singer, spoke up in a penetrating, musical voice. "There's been a new arts programme on that, for the last three weeks. It's supposed to cover arty people and events: has a bit of music and something bookish every week."

"When's it on?" carolled Christobel Templeton (poet, and always on the lookout for a good rhyme for the word "purple").

"Fridays at three o'clock," Fiona announced to anyone who was interested.

"What station?"

"Radio Carsfold."

"Who's the presenter?" Sadie Palister had now given her full attention to Fiona.

"I can't remember his name, but he's quite outspoken on behalf of villages and their inhabitants." Fiona had obviously been paying attention over the past few weeks. Climbing down from her supported plank, the singer flicked on the tea-urn and prepared to inform and educate. "As I said, it's only been on for three weeks, and maybe he'd be glad of the material, as he's only just starting up. It could be a win-win situation for both parties."

"That's as may be, but you say he's outspoken — about what in particular?" interrupted Camilla Markland, harpist and local harpy, and a twenty-four carat bitch in many people's opinion.

Undeterred, Fiona started to recite the contents of the first trio of broadcasts. "Well, the first week he had a go at incomer-commuters, who have raised local house prices over the years, thus making it difficult for real locals to afford to buy properties in the villages."

There was a muted "Hurrah!" from an unusually subdued Ashley Rushton, there with his partner Delia Jephcott, and still suffering from a humongous hangover after celebrating his birthday rather more vigorously than he had intended the night before.

"What do you mean, Ashley?" queried Jeremy Templeton.

"We're incomer-commuters ourselves," Ashley replied, but still in quiet tones, so as not to wake the little men with pick-axes who had taken up residence inside his head. "It's us who've put the house prices up, so I say 'hurrah' for us', for increasing our original invest-ments."

"Point taken," Jeremy conceded with a self-satisfied smile, as the answer hit home.

"The second programme," Fiona continued undeterred, but with a slight frown of irritation gathering on her forehead, "was about the number of buildings in villages which have been converted or totally refurbished and modernised. He said that that was destroying local history."

Again she was interrupted, this time by Minty Wingfield-Heyes, abstract artist. "Bollocks!" she shouted. "If it wasn't for people like us, this particular village would either be a museum, or a ghost town. We've saved it from disappearing into the earth whence it came," she finished, rather pompously.

This received a cheer from all present, but Minty sent the ball straight back to Fiona. "And the third week? He sounds all right so far — a bit of a precious prat, but we can use him for publicity if he's naïve enough to think that places like this could have survived without outside money."

"That was to do with weekenders . . ."

"What? That dreary soap opera the BBC will persist in broadcasting?" Sadie was absolutely not a fan.

"No, you fool! Weekenders who come down to their holiday homes and bring all their food and drink with them — everything with which to pander to their every whim, and never buy anything from the village shops. He also had a go at the aforementioned incomers who shop at the big supermarkets in the surrounding towns. Apparently *we* are 'killing the local economy'. *We're* the reason that village shops are closing down in their droves."

"Huh! Who needs that pathetic bunch of shops in the High Street?" Sadie Palister was on a roll today. "There's not one of them worth a light, as far as everyday living goes. Who'd miss them if they weren't there?"

"The organic foods are very useful for a healthy diet. I wouldn't like to be caught short without bulgar wheat

— or bran — and have to traipse all the way to a supermarket just to get it," Christobel Templeton offered, timidly.

"But you wouldn't *die* without it for a few days, would you?" Sadie Palister persisted. "They do all that healthy stuff in the supermarkets, *and* you can have it delivered."

"I know, but it's not the same, is it? It's so nice to be able to look at, and touch and smell your food before you buy it, don't you think?"

"Not with fresh fish, it isn't." Sadie had an answer for everything, and that seemed to close that particular part of the discussion.

"Well, shall we ask him, then?" Fiona Pargeter brought them back to the crux of the matter.

"Ask him what?" Ashley Rushton was still feeling rough, and hadn't been paying attention, because his insides, feeling like the Bay of Biscay in a force nine, were commandeering his entire concentration.

"Oh, keep up, Ashley!" barked Fiona. "Ask him to report on *our* Arts Festival. He could say a few words about when it's on, on this Friday's programme, and he'd have the weekend to look around and get something for his next programme. What do you think, guys?"

A "yes" in unison answered her question and, at this happy juncture, they all abandoned their various positions and painting materials, and adjourned to the tea-urn for some well-earned refreshment, thoroughly puffed-up with self-importance at their generosity and largesse towards this as-yet unnamed and unsuspecting radio broadcaster.

II

Later that evening, many of the locals were gathered in the saloon bar of The Inn on the Green in eager discussion about the forthcoming Arts Festival. Around one table were gathered Lydia Culverwell the pianist, Delia Jephcott the flautist, and Camilla Markland the harpist. It was tonight's "musical" table.

Around an adjacent table were clustered Sadie Palister, Minty Wingfield-Heyes, Christobel Templeton, Fiona Pargeter, and Felicity Westinghall. (Hugo was at home, ostensibly to look after the children; in reality, to put in a little more practice for his reading the next weekend.) Apart from Fiona, who was blatantly avoiding the company of her neighbour Lydia, this was the "literary and visual arts" table.

Back at the musical table Camilla was sharpening her claws. "No Ashley tonight, Delia?" she asked. "He's such a youngster. I'd have thought he would want to come out of an evening, instead of staying inside like someone middle-aged." (Meow!)

"I freely confess that he's a little younger than me," (he was twenty-eight to her forty-three, but that was by-the-by), "but he doesn't have the stamina that those of us of a slightly more mature persuasion enjoy. Anyway, he's still suffering from the hangover he spent so long courting last night at his birthday celebrations. He was as sick as a dog when we got home from the

14

hall earlier, and when I suggested he might come out for a restorative glass or two, he turned positively green and headed straight for the bathroom again."

"OK, don't get your knickers in a twist. I was just asking, wasn't I?"

"Maybe. But at least I don't lie about *my* age," muttered Delia, under her breath.

"What was that?"

"Oh, nothing; just clearing my throat."

"He probably doesn't need as much stamina as I've had to call on recently," stated Lydia Culverwell cryptically.

"Why's that, old bean? Got yourself a nice fit young bit of bum to keep you warm of a night?" called Sadie Palister, shamelessly eavesdropping from the next table.

Ignoring this interruption, Lydia continued, "It's the constant noise nuisance from next door that's really been getting me down. I was wondering if I could have some time before the Festival opens, to practise in the hall, away from all the discordant distractions."

There was a shouted exclamation in response to this, much louder than all the other voices in the bar, and from the direction of the other table. "I heard that!" retorted Fiona Pargeter.

"You were meant to!" Lydia called back. "If anyone has to put up with noise pollution, it's me, with you "ah-ah-ahing" away all day, out of tune and in the wrong key. It's like living next door to a cats' home. Why don't you just have some singing lessons, and then move to Land's End or John O'Groats to practise?"

Lydia Culverwell vented her spleen with all the accuracy of a trained sniper.

"I heard that, too!" retorted Fiona.

"Good!"

"You spiteful old witch!" (Lydia was a mere two years older than Fiona, thirty-six years to thirty-four — hardly a chasm. But all was fair in love and village war.) "What do you think it's like for me, with you crashing and banging about on that bloody piano of yours, all day, every day. It's like living next to a . . . a . . . a bloody poltergeist!" So great was her anger that Fiona spluttered to find a suitable comparison.

Peregrine McKnight, one half of the management of The Inn on the Green, appeared suddenly between the two warring tables, and offered an olive branch. "I don't know! Such artistic temperaments! Now, why don't we just calm down, and I'll bring you all drinks on the house, to seal a pact of peace. We can't have the law in here, arresting you all for disorderly conduct, can we? Where would our Arts Festival be without you?"

At this exact moment, his partner in management, Tarquin Radcliffe, oozed over with a large tray of drinks, appeasement writ all over his smarmy face. "Here we are, my darlings. Drink, drink, and fight no more. Smile, be happy, and accept our little gift of good luck to you all."

The mood lightened after just a couple of scowled glances, and a voice that had been previously drowned out by the outbreak of hostilities was lifted again in suggestion. "Why don't you just borrow the key to the hall and practise there? As far as I know, Serena

16

Lyddiard is key-holder at the moment. No doubt, she too would like to go in, to get a bit of practice. There can't be much room in her house for dancing, and she'll need to get the feel of the space before her performance." The sweet voice of reason came, unusually, from Delia Jephcott. Normally a dissenting character, she felt she had already got her money's worth tonight, and was more interested in staying out late to annoy Ashley than in going home early after a row.

This final suggestion effectively separated both tables and turned them back in on themselves, as other minds wondered about borrowing the key from Serena and having a little time to themselves, to "try out the acoustics" (aka show off), and plotting how soon they could nip off to Blackbird Cottage to get their hands on this powerful piece of metal.

Those at the musical table, inevitably, left first, closely followed by Fiona Pargeter, whose mind was running along identical lines. At the literary (and visual arts) table, Felicity Westinghall and Christobel Templeton were also anxious to be off, as they had similar aspirations for their recitations, and soon made their farewells, leaving just Sadie and Minty to finish off the pork scratchings. "Ah, what a thing it is, to be spiritual enough to dedicate one's life to one's Art," smirked Sadie to her companion.

"Quite!" agreed Minty Wingfield-Heyes, grinning back, "but only if you can get your sticky little hands on that key, and bag most of the time available for yourself. Thank God we're both exhibiting from home, or we'd probably be scratching each other's eyes out to secure the most prominent positions for our work."

"Amen to that," murmured Sadie. "A-bloody-men to that!"

CHAPTER
TWO

Wednesday, 2nd September

I

It was Fiona Pargeter who took it upon herself to get in touch with Radio Carsfold to obtain the name of the lucky radio presenter, and instructions for getting in touch with him. As it was she who had listened to the programmes, and she who had told everyone else about them, she felt it was her duty to do so (apart from the fact that her melodious speaking voice might possibly be broadcast across the countryside for the enjoyment of others).

The name she was given was "Marcus Willoughby"; the telephone number, another Carsfold one. Fiona's hand displayed a minor tremble as she dialled it, but immediately stopped as a voice answered her summons. It was a deep voice, a deep, golden voice — rich, velvety and suntanned, and she was immediately enchanted. If anyone was going to be tall, dark and handsome, it had to be this man, she thought, automatically putting her hand to her hair. "Hello, is that Marcus Willoughby? Oh, enchanting to speak to you, too. I wonder if I could

19

ask you the teensy-weensiest little favour?" she enquired, making her voice deep and husky — what she thought of as her "sexy" voice.

"And what might that be, dear lady? Speak, and I shall positively rush to your aid."

"Oh! Well, thank you." Fiona was definitely flustered. "It's just that we're putting on — I mean, the village where I live is putting on an Arts Festival, this Saturday and Sunday, actually, and I've been listening to your programmes — so interesting and uplifting — and I wondered if you might . . ." Here, she lost herself a little, but battled on bravely. "I wondered if you might come along to it, might even give it a mention this Friday, and then come along . . . Yes, just come along to it and maybe, oh, I don't know, maybe you could do a few itsy-bitsy minutes on it when you'd seen some of it. I mean, it goes on all weekend, but I couldn't expect . . ."

"Say no more, dear lady. Now, just let me get this straight — there's going to be an Arts Festival in your village?"

"Yes."

"And it's going to be this weekend. That is, the fifth and sixth of this month?"

"Yes."

"And you'd like me to mention it on this week's show, to help with publicity and attendance, no doubt?"

"Yes."

"And to come along in person to report on it?"

"Yes." Fiona had never been at such a loss for words.

"I should be delighted, my dear, provided that you furnish me with three things."

"What?" asked Fiona, even more flustered now.

"Why, the name of the village concerned, the name of your delightful self, and your telephone number, so that I can get in touch with you again about arrangements."

"Oh, of course, how silly of me! And you mentioned the days that I mentioned . . ." She still had not pulled herself together.

"I should be delighted to visit on both days, if you would so desire. Now, tell me about the arts to be represented, and I shall have some idea of what I am up against," he finished, preparing to take notes.

She replaced the receiver of the telephone some twenty minutes later, quite breathless from being charmed. Patting her hair once more and rolling her lips together to make sure her lipstick was still evenly applied, she smiled to herself in self-importance, and prepared to pass on this wonderfully exciting news to the others.

II

"Hello, Serena, guess what?" Serena Lyddiard was not in the mood for guessing games and said so, without preamble, having been badgered almost out of her wits by people "just calling" to see if they could borrow the key of the village hall.

"Oh, all right, it's just that I've been speaking to that radio presenter . . ."

"What radio presenter?"

"Oh, of course, you weren't there. Well, he does a programme on Radio Carsfold called "The Village Culture Vulture" every Friday at three, and I've hunted him down," another unconscious pat at the hair, "*and* I've only got him to agree to advertise our little Festival this Friday, and to turn up in person, both Saturday and Sunday, so that he can fully cover everything." She purred to a halt.

"Who is he?" Serena wasn't really interested, but realised she had been a bit uncharitable when answering the call, and had better get herself up to snuff before she hurt Fiona's feelings.

"Marcus Willoughby."

"Never heard of him!" Whoops, manners slipping again.

"Well, he sounded just divine on the phone. I bet he's well fit. Anyway, thought I'd just let you know, and that it's all down to little old me."

"Well done. Now, if you don't mind, I've got a cake in the oven, and it smells like it's catching."

Fiona heard the receiver replaced, and shrugged. You couldn't please all of the people all of the time. Reclaiming her good mood, she looked at her list of numbers, and began to dial the next one.

III

On one of the benches on the village green, Rev. Benedict Ravenscastle was sitting next to an elderly woman who held a Yorkshire terrier by a slender lead. They were deep in conversation, the subject quite obviously a serious one. "I realise that you miss Bubble very much, and so does little Squeak." He cast a glance at the tiny dog, lifting its leg at the end of the bench. "But he's been gone for over five months now, and I really think that you should put it to the back of your mind, and not depress yourself any more, my dear Squirrel."

Harriet Horsfall-Ertz, a staunch church-goer for all of her seventy-eight years (for she had been carried to church as a babe in arms by her parents) turned her rheumy eyes towards God's representative here on earth (for the parish of Stoney Cross, at least) and said, "But it's this thing with the soul, you see, and the Church thinking that animals don't have them; so what's going to happen to me when I get to the Pearly Gates, and there ain't a little Yorkie capering around, all excited to see me again?"

Still amazed at his audacity in using this elderly woman's nickname, well chosen, as she was an avid carbooter and inveterate hoarder, Rev. Ravenscastle stared wistfully towards the heavens, as if in search of inspiration, absent-mindedly running his right hand over his white hair. "I think, myself, that that is a little harsh of the Church, and if you would like my personal opinion . . ."

"Yes, please, Vicar."

"I think that our pets, like children, bring us such joy, that it would be impossible for God to exclude them from His kingdom. I feel confident that you and Bubble and Squeak, in the fullness of time, will all be together again."

The smile that greeted this pronouncement was so full of relief and happiness, that he patted the old lady's hand kindly, and rose to return to his duties. It may not be what he *should* have said, but it was what he *needed* to say to start the healing process, even this belatedly.

Squirrel greatly missed Squeak's brother, who had been killed on the road in Carsfold in the early dark of March, and she had not been the same person since. Maybe she would begin to pick up a bit again, especially with all the excitement of the Festival. She used to love to be out and about with her little dogs. Maybe she would return to this pastime with her one remaining dog, a little more comforted.

IV

Fiona hung up on the last of her triumphant telephone calls. Apart from Serena Lyddiard, she had spoken to Delia, Camilla, Sadie, Christobel, Felicity (and Hugo, who insisted on grabbing the receiver) and Minty — she, Fiona, was definitely the heroine of the hour. And now she must practise, but at least it would be in peace, for a while. That bitch Lydia Culverwell had beat her to the key last night by dint of leaving the pub just a little bit earlier than her, and positively running to Blackbird Cottage. Absolutely no shame, that woman; and, anyway, she herself had been wearing high-heeled shoes, and could not keep pace with her adversary.

Well, at least with Madam out of the way in the village hall, she could really let rip with her own practice, as loud as she wanted, with no fear of interruption, and she'd have her turn as arranged — the chance to hear her voice soar through all that space, instead of being swallowed by the small areas of domestic living. Perhaps she would go on to the landing, where she knew there would be better acoustics, due to the staircase and hall.

V

At Blacksmith's Cottage, Camilla Markland was in full venomous flight, taking out all her rage and frustrations on her long-suffering husband Gregory, who had unwittingly phoned her in his lunch hour to see how her day was going. (The fool should have known better!)

"You know it's only three days to my first recital, and I've only managed to bag half an hour, and that was by absolutely begging; and that's on Friday, and that's between those two awful warring women from Dragon Lane."

"But you don't want your harp there at the moment. You know you don't like it being moved too much, and it would be so inconvenient if you had to go over there every time you wanted to run through your piece." These were wise words, but they fell on ears deafened by fury.

"That's beside the bloody point! And you know what will happen, don't you? I'll get over there dead on time, and the first one will over-run on purpose to rob me of valuable minutes, and the other one will arrive early and want to get in, and you know how long it takes me to set everything up just so. I simply won't be able to find the right mood, and it'll be a complete waste of time. And, with the harp there, I won't be able to do any last minute practice, and I shall make an absolute fool of myself in front of everybody, and I just want to die." She burst noisily into tears, and hung up on her husband, rushing upstairs to sob in peace in the privacy of her bedroom, pushing her other niggling worry to the back of her mind. She'd have to deal with that "on the hoof", as it were.

VI

From the open windows of The Old School, gusty laughter was carried away on the breeze. Inside the building were Sadie and Minty, the latter having arrived a couple of hours earlier clutching a brace of bottles of chilled Chardonnay. She was feeling a little "windy" about opening her home to strangers, and fancied a bit of a girlie-artist night with a friend. This was not, of course, the first time she had been part of an Artists Trail, but it was her first time from The Old Mill — it was a sort of "loss of virginity" moment for the place.

Sadie had welcomed her with open arms, having already consumed several cans of lager, and by the time they had polished off the wine, they were in a high old mood. "What about all that business in The Inn last night?" called Sadie, her voice muffled by the interior of the fridge, where she was in search of an unfinished bottle or two of wine, to prolong their night.

"I know! Unbelievable!" called back Minty, squinting into her glass to make sure that there wasn't even a tiny drop left to drink.

"What a pack of two-faced bitches some of them are." Sadie's voice grew in volume as she left the kitchen clutching the necks of two bottles, both of them over half full.

"Oh, more drinky-poos!" exclaimed Minty, clapping her hands like a little girl on Christmas morning. It didn't seem to matter how many calories she consumed — she never put on an ounce of weight, and was, fortunately, happy with her slightly padded figure. "Li'l Minty loves her din . . . drinky-poos," a slight slur indicated that she might have had enough already, but was game for a few more glasses before she finally threw in the towel.

"White or white?" Sadie asked, squinting drunkenly at the labels' and giggling as she set the bottles on the table.

"White, I think, with just a li'l bit o' white," Minty replied, with a definite snigger at her own staggering wit. "Goo' frien's, tha's wha' we are, innit, Sadie? We're goo' frien's."

Tottering towards her visitor, slopping wine from the two brim-full glasses she carried, Sadie's face took on a delighted look of mischief. "Yeh! And goo' frien's oughter share secre's, di'n' they?"

"Oo, winey-poos for Li'l Minty. Hic! Yeh, they oughter share . . . wassnames."

Sadie, peering through one half-closed eye at her friend, cocked a finger towards her studio and led Minty to a cloth-covered lump of stone about eighteen inches high. "Woss 'at?" the abstract artist asked, draining her so recently refilled glass at a gulp.

"'M gonna tell you a story. 'Bout some old geezer who too' the pisssss." The sibilant hiss went on a little too long, confirming her similarly inebriated state. "'E reckon ... reckoned my work was rubb'sh. Silly ol' sod! So I made this li'l thingummy for 'im. Loo'! I'll show you!" And with that she whipped the cloth away, staggering several crab-like steps to her left, and laughing again, one hand over her mouth to stifle her glee.

What was revealed caused Minty to gasp, then burst into peals of delighted drunken laughter, her right index finger pointing at the sculpture in disbelief. What had been revealed was a large penis, the lower half erect, the upper half drooping, turning it into the semblance of an inverted "U". The pubic hair was expertly represented, but there were no testes.

"Whereza balls, Sadie? Whereza bollox?"

"Ain't got 'ny."

"Well, wossit called?"

"Art Critic," Sadie pronounced, carefully and precisely. "Iss that geezer wot rubb'sh'd m' work."

"Hee hee hee! Wozz 'is name?"

"Can ... can't 'member atta momen'. Tell you la'er."

Minty took another look at the small sculpture and laughed so hard she wet herself a little, then, finding this fact absolutely hilarious, laughed even harder.

The church clock chimed midnight.

The signs were not auspicious for a bright and early start the next morning for Sadie Palister and Araminta Wingfield-Heyes.

VII

A little earlier, in The Inn on the Green, trade had been far from brisk, due to the fact that everyone involved in the Festival was at home, either titivating their contributions or practising their party pieces. A few customers chatted in a desultory manner, scattered around the old oak tables, but the bar itself was quiet.

"Do you reckon we're going to do a lot of extra trade over the weekend?" Tarquin Radcliffe asked his business partner Peregrine McKnight, "Because, if we do, I reckon we're going to need an extra pair of hands."

"I reckon you're right, old chap. Got any ideas?"

"Well, there was that Doidge dame — what was her name?"

"Suzie."

"That's right. Lived over in King George III Terrace. Do you want me to give her a ring and see if she can come in?"

"Why not?"

"OK! She was a good little worker when she was here at Christmas — bags of experience, and just got on with things. I'll slip out the back and do that then." And Tarquin headed out to the rear of the building to do just that.

He returned after only a couple of minutes. "Not just 'no answer', but the line doesn't seem to be in service any more, so maybe she could do with the money, if she's been cut off."

"Hello, Vicar," called Peregrine, to a figure who had just walked through the door, and beckoned him to approach the bar.

"I haven't come in for a drink, I'm afraid, Mr McKnight. I just called in to have a word with one of my wardens whose wife said he was in here."

"That's all right, Vicar. I'd just like to pick your brains about one of your parishioners, if you don't mind."

"Not at all, so long as it's not confidential. Fire away." Reverend Ravenscastle's face took on a slightly hunted expression as he said this.

"The thing is, we've just tried to contact Suzie Doidge from King George III Terrace, and her phone line seems to be disconnected. Do you know if she's OK?" Tarquin put the question, as he had been the one who had tried to telephone.

"Actually, I don't. Know, that is. It would seem that she's left the area. I think it was in the spring, but I can't be sure. She wasn't one of my regular worshippers, you know, but I try to keep in touch with what's going on, even for those who feel no need to visit the Lord's house."

"Thanks very much, Rev.," put in Peregrine. That was about as much of the "God" stuff as he could take. "I think the gentleman you're looking for is over there by the window playing dominoes." Ravenscastle turned and ambled away, and Peregrine and Tarquin looked at each other, then had to hide their faces as they began to giggle.

"What about Annie Symons, over at Castle Farthing?" Peregrine suggested. "She did a spot of filling in when you had your ingrowing toenail done.

I've got her number in the book by the telephone. Won't be a min."

He also returned with nothing positive. "No answer on the phone, so I gave The Fisherman's Flies a tinkle — you know George and Paula Covington, don't you? She used to give them a hand sometimes — handy-like, with her just being in Drovers Lane — but no joy there. George reckons she moved away to live with a sick relative, and Paula thinks she packed off to Australia to live with a cousin of hers. Whatever, she isn't around any more."

"When do they reckon she went?"

"Not really sure. Before the summer they think, maybe late spring."

"Just our luck! You can't get the staff, you know," Tarquin stated, and stared into space, thinking.

"Something'll turn up, just you wait and see. And after all, it's just a couple of days." This was Peregrine's last word on the matter for now, as he stepped forward to serve an impatient customer who was tapping noisily on the bar with a £2 coin and pointedly clearing his throat.

CHAPTER
THREE

Friday, 4th September — daytime

I

It was early afternoon, and Stoney Cross was abuzz with activity. Some of the local artists were packing up their exhibits ready to be taken to the village hall, others, more astute, were already in the hall, busily bagging the best of the display space. Large heavy screens, like room dividers, had been set up, at right angles to the two long walls. Between these, in the clear through-space, chairs were to be placed to make comfortable those who came to listen to the readings and music to be performed, and watch Serena Lyddiard dance.

At the rear of the hall, at the opposite end to the performing area, trestle tables had been erected, and crockery and tea and coffee urns were being placed thereon, ready for those hungry and thirsty for more than the arts. The tea shop was providing the sandwiches, cakes and biscuits at a discount rate, and this particular catering venture, it was hoped, would provide a good profit for the church restoration fund.

Reverend Ravenscastle and his wife Adella were in attendance at this activity, as was Squirrel Horsfall-Ertz and her inevitable companion, Squeak. His lead secured to the legs of one of the trestle tables, he had crawled beneath this shelter, and now slept peacefully through all the chaos, curled into a tiny furry ball.

Sadie Palister was there to help, having recovered from her over-indulgences of the night before, and her deep voice could be heard booming across the centre section of the hall. "Mrs Solomons, will you please stop taking down Mrs Carstairs' oil paintings and replacing them with your own watercolours. There's plenty of display space for all."

"But I want mine *here*, in the light. They're delicate works, watercolours, and must be hung with care as regards the lighting. Her oils are much gaudier — they could go anywhere and be noticed."

"That's what *she* says," retorted Mrs Carstairs, suddenly becoming aware of what was going on. "I don't know about 'delicate', but it's first come, first served, as far as I'm concerned. Don't you agree Ms Palister?" There was a degree of sucking-up in the final question, but Sadie ignored it, more interested in justice than getting caught in the cross-fire.

"Mrs Solomons, I'm afraid you'll just have to take your watercolours back down and let Mrs Carstairs have that space . . ."

"But . . ."

"No buts! I'm compiling a catalogue for the viewers, and all the screens are numbered, as you can see. If you move Mrs Carstairs' paintings, not only will the viewers not know where hers are, but they won't know who yours are by, when they do find them." This was not strictly true, as the exhibits wouldn't be listed in order until after all of them had been hung, but it was a pretty clever way to stop the in-fighting.

"I suppose you think you're clever, don't you?" sneered Lionel Fitch, eyeing up the disputed space, his pastel works in a tidy pile at his feet.

"Yes, as a matter of fact I do," Sadie replied, then muttered under her breath, "And there's no point whatsoever in making that sign at me, or that face, Mr Fitch. You'd better take care the wind doesn't change, otherwise it'll be awfully difficult for you to shave yourself in the morning," she threatened, voice raised once more.

II

Minty Wingfield-Heyes had awoken with one of those hangovers that go through two stages. At first, you just wish you could die, you feel so awful. Then, as you get up and about, the second stage sets in; the one where you wish you had died, because *nothing* could be worse than this.

At first she had *felt* as sick as a dog; then she *was*. Two cups of black coffee and a piece of dry toast also made an encore appearance, and it wasn't until after a really long, hot shower, and two painkillers, that she felt human enough to get dressed and give breakfast another try, this time with a little more success. Never again, she vowed, would she get that drunk. Never again! If she hadn't woken up at all that morning, it would probably have been a relief, the way she had felt.

Feeling slightly more human, she decided to take a stroll — slowly — down to the village hall and see how everything was going. She had left her house ready for inspection the previous evening, when she had gone over to Sadie's, and if she kept herself out of it, it would stay that way until tomorrow, when those on the Artists Trail would (she hoped) start to arrive.

It wasn't just she and Sadie who had decided to display at home, a few others — mainly the more untrusting artists who were the most covetous of their handiwork — had taken the opportunity to display from home as well, and there would be a little map prepared, showing the houses participating, the artist, and the type of work on display.

As she approached The Old Barn she became aware that there was a large removals lorry parked outside, partially blocking the roadway, and an unknown car in the drive. It was a Tuscan TVR with a personalised number-plate — R7 MEW, and she wondered whose it was. The Old Barn had stood empty for some months, and it now appeared that, during this time, it had found a new owner.

Her curiosity was soon to be satisfied for, at the rear of the removals truck, peering helplessly through its open doors, was the figure of a compact and rather elderly gentleman. Bidding him good morning, and asking if she had the pleasure of addressing the village's newest resident, Minty offered her hand. At the sound of her voice, the figure turned and fixed her with his blue eyes, smiling out from behind a pair of rimless glasses.

Taking her hand and, instead of shaking it, raising it to his rather thin lips, he kissed it. "Marcus Willoughby at your service, delightful young lady." His face seemed to radiate bonhomie as he said this, and Minty did a split-second job of sizing him up. "About five-eight," she thought, "white hair, number five cut; silly little triangle of bristle beneath his bottom lip; just beginning to paunch up and go to seed a bit; oh, and a gold stud in his left ear. And I believe he's probably a bit of an old flirt; thinks he's charming."

She took in these details so quickly that there was hardly a hesitation before she returned his smile and withdrew her hand slightly uncomfortably, resisting the urge to wipe the back of it on her cardigan sleeve. "Aren't you that radio chappie?" she asked, his name finally ringing a loud and urgent bell in her mind.

"The very same: Marcus Willoughby, otherwise known as the 'Village Culture Vulture' — stalwart of Radio Carsfold," he informed her, slightly exaggerating his importance, but not giving a fig.

"Then you must be the one who's going to cover our little village Festival."

"Absolutely right, dear lady, and I believe it opens tomorrow."

"That's right, but they're setting up at the moment. Would you like to come and have a look and, maybe, a cup of tea? I should think you're parched, with all this moving lark, what? Or am I disturbing you — I'm so sorry. I'll leave you in peace to get on with whatever you were going to do."

"Not at all, not at all. I was just looking for the box with my kettle and tea and coffee things in it, but, as I can detect neither hide nor hair of it, lead on — lead on, and make an old man very happy," he replied, and, tucking her right arm snugly under his left so that he would be on the road side of the little pavement, he led her down towards the High Street towards the village hall.

"What a dreadful old smarm-pot," she thought, as she bobbed along at his side, all thoughts of her hangover completely forgotten. "I can't wait to show him off to Yodelling Fiona — she'll have a cow. Tall, dark and handsome, my arse!"

III

They entered the village hall to the strains of a loud and emotional argument being carried out at the front of the hall in the performance area, several voices raised in acute and angry distress.

"You've hogged most of the practice time this week, you selfish bitch, and I need to get my instrument set up to try the acoustics." This was Camilla Markland, and she yelled this in defence of her harp, which was now in place, next to where she stood in combat.

"No I haven't, you stupid old witch," Lydia Culverwell screamed back at her. "I've hardly been able to set foot in here due to Fiona bloody Pargeter, who

37

can't seem to sing at home because of her interrupting, needy little brats."

"Hang on a *minute*," shrilled Fiona Pargeter. "Firstly, how *dare* you say that my kids are brats. They are exceptionally well-behaved, and they are *not* needy. And secondly, don't you dare blame *me* for taking up all the time in the hall. Delia's been here too, with her flute; Felicity, Christobel, and Hugh have all been here practising their readings, and Serena's been here too, running through her dance routine. Haven't you dear?" she finished, making an appeal for support to Serena Lyddiard, who had been patiently waiting her turn for control of the performance area, but was now nowhere in sight.

"I couldn't give a shit if the Archbishop of bloody Canterbury has been in here pole-dancing. I need to practise, and I need to practise *now*." Camilla had undoubtedly won the fight she had been spoiling for, having being prepared, if necessary, for hair-pulling, face-scratching bloody war.

"Oh, get stuffed, you foul-mouthed cow!" Fiona threw her final squib, and marched away from the battlefield, only to run, full-tilt, into Minty Wingfield-Heyes, who had a slimy-looking old git in tow.

"Good afternoon, Fiona, and how are we today?" Minty positively trilled, as she disengaged her arm from her companion's and prepared to make introductions.

"Bloody awful, if you must know. And who's this? If it's some other artist looking for space, there is none; and, what's more, he should have called weeks ago, and not left it to the very last minute," she trumpeted indignantly; she had no time for people who didn't plan ahead.

"No, no, Fiona, you're very much in the wrong. May I introduce you to Marcus Willoughby? Mr Willoughby, this is Mrs Fiona Pargeter, to whom, if I am not mistaken, you have already had the pleasure of speaking, on the telephone."

Fiona's face drained of colour, her mouth gaped, and her eyes popped, as if in an effort to follow her lower jaw. Her embarrassment was fortunately, however, short-lived, as someone at the rear of the hall had turned up the volume to maximum on a radio that had been murmuring away to itself for some time. Marcus's voice could be heard, booming around the enclosed space, announcing the forthcoming Arts Festival in Stoney Cross, which would commence on the morrow.

As the broadcast droned on, lamenting the demise of village businesses and rural bus services, all, in the broadcaster's opinion, due to commuters, incomers, weekenders and supermarket giants, and was superseded by Verdi's "Dies Irae", chosen by the presenter as piece number one in today's edition of his show, many who had been listening returned to their previous activities, and the low buzz of conversation began to swell in volume.

Above all the noise, however, was a thought — a thought in so many minds, that it should have boomed above all the chatter. "No! It *can't* be! Not after all this time!"

IV

A number of people had left the hall before Minty could continue with her introductions. Delia Jephcott had put her flute away in its case and left by the back exit door, excusing herself by saying she would get much more practice done if she went home, but she looked slightly shifty as she gave her reason for departing.

Camilla Markland, after a hasty glance in Minty's direction, turned beetroot-red and abandoned the battle, slinking away from her beloved harp and heading in the same direction that Delia had. She felt nauseous and shocked, and wanted nothing more than to retreat home to get her thoughts in order.

Serena Lyddiard had also made her exit before Marcus could be properly introduced, making her exit shortly after the radio programme had started to boom round the hall. She was at home now, swathing her right ankle and heel in bandages. She couldn't dance now, not after what had just happened. She'd better leave a message on Fiona's answerphone telling her that, as she had sprained her ankle quite severely, she could not perform. That was the best plan — after all, she didn't want them running round here when they had so much to do before tomorrow.

Even the vicar's wife had joined the general exodus after she had been introduced to Marcus, finding her husband and informing him that she had a sick headache, and wanted to lie down in a darkened room before it developed into a full-blown migraine. She looked so pale and wretched that her husband agreed with her, and shooed her off anxiously, promising to bring her a cup of mint tea when he got home.

Adella Ravenscastle moved with surprising speed for one in her condition, but her pace was just trying to keep up with her thoughts. She knew that face. She could never forget that face. What on earth was she going to say to her sister, Meredith? How was she going to explain to her sister that the man who had mown down her only daughter (Adella's ten-year-old niece, Maria), was actually in Stoney Cross? That he was now resident in Benedict's parish? And what would Benedict say when he saw the man again, and realised why she had left so precipitously?

How would she ever be able to look *that man* in the face, without him seeing the hatred in her eyes? She knew that Benedict would ask her to search her heart for forgiveness, but she couldn't; she just couldn't. It was nearly eight years ago now, but it still disturbed her sleep and haunted her dreams. She might be wicked for not forgiving him, but how much more wicked was he, in that he had taken an innocent life, and just carried on living his own? She really did have a headache now, and headed straight for the bedroom when she reached The Vicarage.

During this busy early period, Marcus had suddenly wheeled round, as his eye had caught the toss of a familiar head, a walk he had thought he recognised. "Hey!" he had shouted. "Hoy!" but there had been no response. Shaking his head sorrowfully, he realised that he must have been mistaken.

But, just for a moment there, he had been so sure.

V

Back in the village hall, Fiona Pargeter had recovered her dignity, had meekly accepted another, more civilised introduction to Maurice Willoughby, and was blustering about improvised drama (to explain the shouting match), and how some of them often had a go at it in public, just to see what reaction they would get. But she was unconvincing, and Minty had to turn away for a moment to wipe away her grin, using her handkerchief as a handy prop. If Fiona could drivel on about non-existent am-dram, then she could use her hanky for a bit of "business".

"You really must excuse our little japes, Mr Willoughby. I suppose some of us can never quite suppress the 'inner child'," Fiona explained, actually using an improvisation of her own, with which to extricate herself from this embarrassing situation. She followed it with an attempt at her tinkling, musical-box laugh [more like an ice-cream van, in my opinion!], but it didn't come off, and had a jarring note in it, as if some of the little metal teeth had become distorted and out of tune.

"Don't give it a second thought, my dear Ms Pargeter. I quite understand," he soothed, while Minty reached, once again, for her handkerchief, as her thoughts ran more along the line of petty playground squabbles, hair-pulling, pinching and biting.

42

"By the way, Mr Willoughby . . ."

"Do call me Marcus."

"Thank you so much, and you must call me Fiona." (She can't think she's got away with it, can she? thought Minty. For sheer, brazen cheek, she certainly took the biscuit.)

"Thank you so much . . . Marcus. I was just wondering, how did you manage to be on the radio just now, when we could see you standing in here? I know things like music are just flicked on, and that can be done by anyone, but it sounded as if you were broadcasting live — no script or anything."

"Simple, my dear," Marcus began, as several pairs of ears pricked up to learn this handy little trick, and it would, no doubt, be common knowledge in every household before the end of the day.

"I use a small recorder to make notes on, if I'm reporting something like this. Then, later, when I can get on to my laptop, I use the scribbled notes I've made, from what I recorded earlier, select a suitable sound programme, and just talk away. I can then convert it to the form necessary for the radio station, send it to them — and just leave them to get on with it."

"But that's ingenious. Not having to show up at a set time or day, no script-writing, and not even a telephone call?"

"And you get paid for this?"

"Correct! Good, isn't it?"

More like money for old rope, thought Minty, and started to steer him round the hall to meet more of his new neighbours in Stoney Cross.

After a few more introductions, Minty realised that the crowd had thinned somewhat, and led the broadcaster to the trestle tables for the cup of tea she had promised him quite some while ago. Adella had already deserted her post, and Rev. Ravenscastle had tottered off with a jug to the cloakroom for more water for the urns. It was, therefore, Squirrel who looked up brightly to see who wanted to be served.

As she looked at her customers, her gaze homed in on Marcus's face, and the smile was wiped from hers, to be replaced with a mask of rage and hatred. "It's you, you bloody old devil! It's you! You killed my Bubble, and I'll have your hide for it, you snivelling cowardly toad." As she finished her tirade, Squirrel had grasped a knife, on the table for the purpose of cutting cakes, and was inching her arthritic form from behind her work station.

Grabbing his arm, Minty fairly galloped out into the open air, pulling him in her wake, and headed in the general direction of The Old Barn. "What was all that about?" he asked, breathless, as she dragged him along.

"Did you ever have an accident in Carsfold where you killed a dog?"

"For a moment, his face was sweatily pallid, but began to regain its colour on the word "dog".

"I'm afraid I did. Quite a few months back, now — I'd forgotten all about it."

"Well, you've just met its owner," puffed Minty. "That little dog was her Bubble, and she's still got his brother, Squeak. I should keep away from dark

44

alleyways, if I were you. Did you see how quick she was picking up that knife?"

"I did; and I will! I really don't fancy getting sliced up for this lot, to be discussed with a refreshing brew while they bitch their way around the exhibits."

"You'd better believe it, brother. It's the truth!"

"I must confess, I didn't think that meeting the neighbours would be such a stressful experience," he admitted, then drooped the lid of his right eye in Minty's direction, in a lazy wink. "But never mind, I expect I'll get over it."

VI

Squirrel Horsfall-Ertz had also fled the hall, shortly after the man she now thought of as "the murderer". Almost dragging Squeak in her wake, she rushed home to Church Cottage, making straight for the back garden, where she knelt, slowly and painfully, beside a little grave with the name "Bubble" lightly scratched on a stone at its head. Drooping her shoulders and letting her head fall forward, she wept, sobbing incoherent threats of revenge and grief.

CHAPTER
FOUR

Friday, 4th September — evening

I

After making one room sane and comfortable, and preparing his bed for the night, Marcus Willoughby strolled
down to The Inn on the Green for some strengthening
refreshment, and a bit more local colour. He had a
feeling he was going to like it here. It hadn't been very
nice when that old hag had had a go at him, but she
looked, to him, like the local nutcase. They should keep
a better eye on her, and not let her near any sharp implements in the future, in his opinion. And he would do
his very best to avoid her if he ever saw her in the street,
he decided with a discernable nod of his head. Apart
from her, he thought he might just have some fun here.

Settling down with his drink, trying to soak up the
atmosphere, he found himself unintentionally listening
in on the conversation of two young women at a nearby
table then, as the conversation progressed, eavesdropping
intentionally. Wasn't this sort of thing meat and drink
to him? Didn't it just breathe life and authenticity into
his programmes? He really fancied himself as an

anecdotist, and was determined to further his public standing in that respect.

"Come on, Trace, yer know why we come on this little holiday — to try and find some rural totty wiv a bit of dosh. How're yer gonna do that if yer don't wear shorts? That was the whole point of the treatments, long, brahn, luscious legs."

"I got it wrong, didn't I, Leeza?"

"'Ow did yer get it wrong? It was simple, wonnit? Leg wax then fake tan."

"I did it the wrong way round, didn't I?"

"The wrong way round?"

"Yeah. I had the fake tan first, then, when they done the waxing, I got all these pale stripes on me legs. I look like a right freak in shorts."

"Yer daft cow, Trace! What about the Brazilian? Yer can't have mucked that up."

"I did, though."

"'Ow?" [These two didn't need a headache, to beg the administration of a couple of "aspirates".]

"I forgot what it was called, mumbled something about maybe it were something Mexican, and the next fing I knew, she'd waxed me top lip white, and made me look even more of a freak. I left then, before I could make fings even worse."

"You stupid cow! I fought there was sumfink funny about yer face."

"Well, I 'ad to put make-up on, didn't I, so as to 'ide the white bit? Otherwise, I'd 've looked like a bloke wiv a very pale moustache. Sorry, Leeze."

"What am I gonna do wiv yer, Trace? How're we gonna find someone fit and loaded, wiv you looking a right stupid bitch?"

At this point, Marcus's chivalrous gene fired up, the rest of him forgot his age, and he rose and approached their table.

"Good evening ladies," he opened, capturing their attention. "I, ah, overheard a little of what you were saying, and I just wanted, ah, you know, to let you know that *I'm* free."

"I'm not surprised, Granddad. You're well past yer sell-by date," the one called Tracey responded, wrinkling her nose in distaste.

"An' you'd better watch out yer don't go past yer use-by date, as well," added the one called Leeza, not wanting to be left out, "or even the worms won't look at yer!" and the two of them started laughing mockingly, pleased with their own wit and youth. Marcus swept up his glass from the table and approached the bar for a refill.

"Common little guttersnipes," he thought, "not at all like the inhabitants of this fair village."

II

Instantly pushing the afore-going incident to the back of his mind, he thought again about earlier. Had he seen whom he thought he had seen? And who was the woman with the honey-coloured hair? He'd have one more drink, he decided, then go home and get an early night, for the Festival opened tomorrow morning, and he wanted his perceptions and his wits to be as sharp as possible.

When Minty left the village hall she didn't head straight for home, but turned right, off the Market Darley Road and into Stoney Stile Lane, making for Blackbird Cottage. Word had got round, as it does in its mysterious way in a village, that Serena Lyddiard had hurt her ankle, and Minty thought it only neighbourly to see if there was anything she could do to help: a little shopping or light housework, time permitting (especially over the weekend, when she was supposed to be on duty in her own house).

She waited for quite some time after ringing the bell and belabouring the knocker, and was just about to turn away, disappointed, when the door slowly opened to reveal Serena, her right ankle and foot swathed in bandages, and a pair of old-fashioned crutches tucked under her arms.

"Well, you poor old crock, you won't be back at work at that nursing home for some time. I can't see you helping the old dears around when you can't even get around yourself."

"Hello, Minty, do come in. Only, if you want tea or coffee, I'm afraid you'll have to make it yourself. I've managed to make myself a flask, but I can't face standing on this ankle any more at the moment, and I must sit down again."

"Don't worry yourself." Minty ushered Serena back to her armchair and headed straight for the kitchen. "What'll it be? Tea or coffee?"

"Oh, tea, please. I've got coffee in my flask, but tea just doesn't seem to survive so well if you bottle it up."

"Quite right! What exactly did you do? It looks rather nasty, the way you're hobbling around."

"The usual silly thing. I wasn't even dancing. I just turned suddenly, and forgot to take my leg with me — then it was 'ow'! — and no more dancing for Serena Lyddiard."

"Oh no!" Minty exclaimed. "Are you sure it won't be better by Sunday afternoon?"

"Not a chance. It's going to take some time for this to heal, and I'm just going to have to sit here and put up with it. I haven't really got a choice, have I?"

"I see what you mean. Is there anything I can do for you — anything that's really urgent, like no loo roll, or something?"

"Nothing like that, but I did leave a message on Fiona Pargeter's answerphone. Perhaps you could just nip round there on your way home and let her know I'm fine, and not to bother coming round, what with the opening of the Festival tomorrow and all that."

"No problem. I'll pop round as soon as we've had this tea. Never fear, Minty's here!"

III

Although Minty had vowed, just that morning, that she would never touch another drop of alcoholic liquor, after speaking to Fiona and being the ear-piece for yet another of her bitching sessions about practice time at the hall, she turned towards The Inn on the Green.

As she walked down the High Street, preparatory to turning left into School Lane, she saw Sadie Palister, also, presumably, on her way to the village watering hole, and she slowed until they could make the last few steps of the journey together. As they approached the pub, Marcus Willoughby exited it, nodding his head slightly in greeting as he passed them.

Both of them slowed their step a little, and they turned to look at each other.

"I think we need a little talk," Sadie opened. "I need to tell you something and, by the look of you, you're going to tell me exactly the same thing. Let's get settled inside, and I'll start the ball rolling."

Once seated at a corner table slightly removed from the other drinkers and, therefore, semi-private, Sadie kept her word, and began to speak in a low voice. "I know that man's face. I just know I've seen it somewhere before. I couldn't think where from, but then something clicked when I got home, and suddenly I needed some Dutch courage before tomorrow, in case history repeats itself."

"I knew his face as well, and there's something nagging at the back of my mind that I can't quite get hold of."

"You said you'd taken part in Artists Trails before. Did you ever have a little card left beside one of your paintings? Not quite a business card, more like an old-fashioned visiting card?"

"Yes! I did!"

"And did your work get a spiteful and severely critical review in the local rag shortly afterwards, with no name attributed to it?"

"Yes! But I can't remember what was on the card. Whatever it was, meant nothing to me. I assumed it had been left behind by accident, and just shoved it in the bin."

"What it had on it were three initials, right? — 'AAL has visited you'. No address or job description, just the three initials."

"Yep," said Minty, "I can sort of see it if I think back hard enough, but have you got any idea what they stand for?"

"I certainly have! They stand for 'Anonymous Art Lover!'," Sadie spat, with contempt. "The card was a pompous little gesture by one of the journalists on the local rag. Thought himself on a level with famous food critics, and always viewed anonymously — no interviews, just a write-up in his usual poisonous vein. Just as well really. If he'd spoken to any of the artists, me included, I'd have smashed his face in for him. I told you I'd been given a rough ride, when I showed you that little sculpture of mine — you remember?" Minty nodded her head, this recollection of her drunken evening unexpectedly vivid.

"Now, Minty, I know you haven't done a Trail in Stoney Cross yet, but cast your mind back to your old house. Just think of his ugly mug, and see if you can place him on the day you found that little card."

After a few moments of silence and a screwed-up face, Minty yelled, "Yes!" and then ducked her head as some of the other customers looked towards their table. "He asked me for a glass of water."

"That's right, me too," whispered Sadie. "That's the little creep who stitched up — I presume — both of us.

I didn't sell anything for months after that, and here I am — here we both are — letting him into our homes again to have another pop at us. I didn't know what to do about it, so I thought I'd get myself a bit of Dutch courage and a think, and then I ran into you, and when we both reacted to seeing him, I realised that we were in the same boat. Have you got any ideas?"

Minty screwed up her face again, and commenced one of her "deep thinks". "I suppose we could shove up the closed sign or lock the door — or simply hide," she suggested, weakly.

"A bit eccentric if there are other viewers in the house, don't you think?"

"Point taken! But, Sadie, oh my God, oh my God, oh my God . . . Your statue — 'Art Critic'. You've got to hide it — you simply have to, or he'll have a hissy fit and absolutely crucify you."

"The statue stays," Sadie pronounced, and drained her glass, sounding braver than she felt.

IV

Back in The Old Barn, Marcus Willoughby sat at his desk surrounded by boxes of books, and made a few notes on his first impressions of Stoney Cross. He had already decided that he would enjoy living here, and he would certainly have some fun with his broadcast, with regard to the forthcoming Festival. He pursed his rather thin lips in spinsterish spite, as he added a few more jottings to his already growing collection.

A tap at the French windows distracted him, and he turned to see the pale orb of a face pressed against one of the panes of glass, which, on opening the doors, resolved itself into that of the girl from the pub — the one with the strawberry-blonde hair — the one he remembered was called Leeza.

With no idea what she wanted with him, he opened the doors and merely stared at her, then asked, "What?" in a rather authoritarian voice. She'd already mocked him and made a fool of him. What more could she want?

"Look, I'm most awfully sorry for what I said earlier . . ." she began, and he simply stared at her in disbelief.

"What the devil's happened to your voice?" he asked, aghast. In The Inn she had sounded so common. Her voice was soft and refined now, with no trace of the dreadful accent of earlier. In fact, she sounded as if she could have gone to the same school as Araminta Wingfield-Heyes.

"Just a cover my friend and I always use when we think we're being listened to. I'm sorry if we hurt your feelings, but sometimes it's rather fun just to run off at the mouth and see what happens." (What was it with this village and improvised drama? he asked himself.) "There's no real offence intended, we were just trying to restore privacy to our conversation, and you must admit that tonight's effort was a belter."

"I rather suppose it was," Marcus admitted.

"And I do really need to talk to you. It's of the utmost importance. If you can forgive me for earlier, and just spare me a few minutes, I should be eternally grateful."

"Of course, of course. Do come in." Marcus was intrigued. "There's space on the sofa, if you'd like to explain yourself a little further, and tell me what all this has to do with me."

"I just want to ask you a few questions — make sure my deductions are correct."

"Your deductions? Fire away!"

"Did you father a daughter in 1985?"

"I really don't see what business that is of yours, young lady!" Marcus almost spat, his face creased in a frown of indignation.

"And did you used to be called Norman Clegg?"

"How dare you . . ."

"I just wanted to be sure before I said anything, because *I'm* your daughter."

Marcus's mouth dropped open in astonishment. How on earth did she know all this?

"That information is not for public broadcast, young lady. I don't know how you have come across it, but I shall deny it absolutely if you say anything about it to a third party."

"I have the information because I've been trying to find you for years. Changing your name didn't help much, but I got as far as Carsfold this afternoon, and turned up on your ex-doorstep. I was directed to Stoney Cross by a neighbour, and thought the pub was as good a place as any, to get a lead on where you had moved to. As it happened, you fell right into my lap — that was just good luck. After I'd seen my friend off, I had one more drink and strolled up here, having gone out the back way and seen where you'd gone to ground."

"If you're my daughter, when were you born, and what's your mother's name?" Marcus could be cunning when he wanted to, and wasn't going to be bled for a penny, if he could help it.

"I was born on the twenty-first of September, nineteen-eighty-five, and my mother's name is Jennifer Linden; always referred to as Jenny, I've been given to understand."

She'd got him, and, admitting genuine defeat, Marcus held out his hand shyly and said, "Delighted to meet you, young lady. It would appear that I *am* your father," then, throwing caution to the wind, he enveloped her in the sort of hug worthy of a long-lost parent.

"Delighted to meet you too . . . Dad. My name's Summer Leighton."

"What a lovely name. So pretty, just like your . . . Just like your mother." His voice softened. "Will you be staying around so that we can get to know one another?" he asked nervously, stepping back from her and hoping fervently that the answer would be "yes". He had never actually wanted her to be adopted, and a sudden thrill rang through him at this belated reunion.

"I've got to get back home for a bit. I'm sorry, but you took some finding. I'm off tonight, but I'll give you all my contact details if you'll give me yours. I'll be in touch, and I promise I'll be back here in a few days' time — I've got some loose ends to tie up before I can

56

spend some quality time with you. And I still haven't found my mother. She seems to have disappeared off the face of the earth the moment I was born."

"Don't you worry about that," Marcus reassured her. "We'll solve that little problem together, you and I."

V

In Blackbird Cottage, Serena Lyddiard sat and looked mournfully at her bandage-swathed ankle. She'd been looking forward so much to performing again — dancing, instead of cleaning, feeding, and hefting around elderly, sick bodies. Granted, she only needed to work part-time, but dancing was her first love, and she had remained true to it throughout her life. So many things had been spoilt for her that she should be used to it by now, but still, she felt the loss of her little public "treat" keenly, and sighed at this most recent defeat.

The last of the light faded away over the village of Stoney Cross, a fitting finale to what had been a spectacular sunset, a virtuoso performance, with its pinks, yellows, blues and purples, that had gone entirely unnoticed by an audience distracted by everyday trivia and their own little problems. Thus is beauty overlooked every day, nature's splendours ignored, as the people below, scurrying little ants, go about their business without a thought to the wonders that surround them.

CHAPTER
FIVE

The next few days in Stoney Cross were fairly eventful, with several unpleasant episodes to mar their passing. These, almost certainly were due to the residents' highly emotional involvement in the Festival, and with Marcus Willoughby playing the part of catalyst. Apart from the usual petty rivalries displayed at such an event, some encounters and conversations were definitely worthy of note.

Saturday, 5th September

I

At The Old Mill, Minty had not slept well, and although her home was spotless, her massive works of art well-displayed, she, herself, was a wreck. She sat on the bottom step of the flight of stairs up to her mezzanine bedroom, drooping with tiredness from her restless night, and screwed up to fever pitch, lest someone should come through the door to view her works — lest it be *him*.

On one occasion, and probably today, that person *would* be Marcus Willoughby, and he had already savaged her work once. That he was a Philistine who simply didn't understand what she did, she was absolutely sure — absolutely sure also, that, even given the chance to explain what she was trying to say in her paintings, it would not change his opinions one whit. If he didn't show a little more mercy this time he could finish off her career, and it had been going so well, with the exception of that little blip, when he had, in the persona of "AAL", mauled her work in the Carsfold Gazette.

II

In The Old School, Sadie Palister was in a similar, if not worse condition. She sat hunched up at her kitchen table over a cup of strong black coffee, her mood flitting between resentment at what AAL had written about her in the past, anxiety about Marcus viewing her more recent works and venting his spleen on them again, this time on the radio, and a thrill of sheer terror mixed with exhilaration, as she imagined him coming across her "special" piece — "Art Critic".

If he was going to rubbish her works and talent, she might as well give him a great big bone to chew on; a giant rubber bone for him to worry at to his heart's content. Just imagining his face as light dawned as to its inspiration, she gave a nervous little giggle, and became aware of a cold slick of perspiration, the product of fear, on her forehead and top lip.

Let him come! she thought. I'm an artist, and he's just an uncultured little prick, trying to bolster up his ego by shredding other people's reputations. His mean-spirited little outbursts only displayed his jealousy of others, because he didn't have an artistic bone in his body. What a poseur! Sadie lit a cigarette, her first in three years, and prepared for battle.

III

The Festival had opened at nine o'clock, and by half-past, Marcus was in the village hall inspecting the visual exhibits. He would attend the musical and literary performances the next day, calling in on those participating in the Trail on his way into the village, thus giving him time to fully digest what he had experienced, and plenty of opportunity to get a nice little piece done for this week's programme.

As he wandered round the screens he sighed, tut-tutted, frowned and muttered into his hand-held recorder. Many exhibits he just passed by, thinking them too insipid and inept even to look at, although they would get a mention to illustrate his dissatisfaction, and the self-delusion of those who thought they were talented.

Mrs Carstairs' oils he dismissed completely out of hand. She had used a palette knife for some, and he chuckled as he thought that, maybe, she should have used a Stanley knife, and been done with it. Mrs Solomons's watercolours he considered a complete waste of good paper and paints. In his opinion, she had no idea whatsoever of perspective, and her range of colours was too washed-out and limited.

The pastels, so lovingly hung by Lionel Fitch, command-ed his complete attention. This artist obviously saw himself as a bit of a modernist, and everything represented in his exhibits was askew and distorted. He must really love pink and purple, Marcus decided, as he viewed the deformed figures and landscapes. Glowering hideously, he began to mutter into his voice recorder, unaware that the figure standing almost by his shoulder was the artist himself, and that he could hear every low-volume word that Marcus uttered.

On his perambulations round the hall, he espied Camilla Markland the harpist, browsing what was on offer. It was true that a few of the pictures sported little red stickers, indicating that they were already sold. There was no accounting for taste, he supposed, and homed in on his victim.

"Hel-*lo*, my dear Camilla," he breathed into her ear, from behind, and was very satisfied with the start that this produced. "And how are we today? Ready for another night of sublime passion? My house is your house, as they say in Spain," he murmured, imagining his voice as irresistibly sexy.

Camilla recovered from her shock and, a little green about the gills, adopted a pseudo-puzzled expression, and replied, "I'm terribly sorry, but I haven't the faintest idea what you're talking about." But her voice shook as she said it.

"Ah," whispered Marcus, with a conspiratorial half-wink. "Our little secret, is it? Hubby doesn't know? Never mind, I shan't breathe a word, as long as we can have a repeat performance in the not-*too*-distant future. What do you say, sexy?"

The harpist visibly swayed on her feet then, recovering her dignity, almost spat at him. "It's been delightful to meet you, Mr Willoughby, but I really must be getting back home." And with that, she turned on her heel and tottered out of the village hall, breaking into a run as she reached Church Lane, her face now bright scarlet, and with tears in her eyes.

What if he said something? What if he tried to force her to do something that would surely make her sick now? How was she going to keep it from her husband Gregory? Would it destroy her marriage? And, even more immediate, how on earth was she going to be able to perform in public tomorrow, knowing that that repugnant old lecher was in the audience leering at her.

Remembering what had happened between them. She had had her Chardonnay goggles on when she had met him last year, after one of her performances, and her mind shied away from the dreadful, disgusting memories of what had occurred that night.

As she left, Marcus had stared after her in a slightly bewildered fashion. She had seemed keen enough when they had last met. So he had been a little pushy, a bit pressuring, mentioning her husband like that — but he had enjoyed the hours they had spent together, and was very anxious to repeat the experience.

Dismissing these thoughts from his mind, his eye alighted on Delia Jephcott, and he ambled suavely in her direction. Here, indeed, was some *big* fun, and he was going to enjoy this encounter to the utmost of his ability.

Delia, over by the refreshment tables and looking almost naked without the presence of her flute, became aware of him as he laid a hand on her arm. Another rear attack, and not quite cricket. Turning round and identifying him, she pulled away as if in disgust, and launched straight into a whispered tirade. "Nobody knows about us. Not even Ashley — my partner. We may have a shared past, but that doesn't mean you own the rest of my life. I'm happy here, and I don't want anything to happen to spoil that."

Marcus smiled at her in mock bewilderment, and slightly lifted his shoulders in a movement, almost Gallic, in its expressiveness.

"I mean what I say, Marcus. Just one word and you'll be sorry. I mean it! If you let the cat out of the bag, I'll wring your worthless neck, I swear I will." Giving him no chance to reply, she marched away to the other end of the hall and left by the emergency exit, still fuming.

Somewhat bewildered by the unfavourable impressions he seemed to be making, he turned towards the refreshment tables for a cheering cup of tea, but before he had completed his turn, he had his cup of tea, boiling hot, and all over his jacket. Dripping, slightly scalded, and burning with anger, he confronted his attacker. "Bloody murdering bastard!" yelled Squirrel, normally so quietly spoken and polite, who then pushed her way through the queue and headed for home.

Mopping at his sodden sleeve with his handkerchief, Marcus decided to call it a day and go home to get something assembled for his next programme. He was just about in the right mood for it now.

A few minutes after he had left, Lionel Fitch's voice rose above the general hum of conversation. "I heard what he was saying into that machine of his, about my pictures — nasty, horrible things; and his face looked evil. I'm fed up to the back teeth with people like him. Who does he think he is, eh? Criticising people for being incomers and commuters, and all the other things His Lordship takes a fancy to having a go at?

"I live here because I bloody-well want to, and because I can bloody-well afford to. Who's he to talk? He only moved here yesterday — incomers, my big fat hairy arse — *And* into a converted barn, when he's slagged-off everyone else who's ever converted an old building. Hypocritical, sanctimonious old bugger! And I damned well *am* a good artist, whatever gobshites like him say!"

IV

Later that evening, Marcus Willoughby picked up his telephone receiver and dialled a number he had ferreted out, with some difficulty, during the course of the day. He had been thinking hard since Summer's unexpected visit yesterday, and was now certain that he was right, and that this was the best course of action. After three rings, his call was answered, and he knew, as soon as the voice spoke, that he had scored a bulls-eye.

"Hello Jenny — no, don't hang up! I know who you are, and there's nothing to be done about that. I just

64

wanted you to know that *our daughter* has been in touch with me, but is mystified as to your whereabouts. I'm ringing to tell you that I believe it to be my moral duty to tell her who and where you are."

The line went dead, as the receiver was slammed down at the other end. "Jenny? Jenny?" Gently replacing his own receiver, Marcus smiled to himself. Sanctimonious old humbug he might be, but he was looking forward to the little contretemps he was about to cause.

CHAPTER
SIX

Sunday, 6th September

I

Marcus Willoughby was whistling quietly on Sunday morning, when he exited The Old Barn and turned right, heading for The Old Mill. He had no idea what awaited him at Araminta Wingfield-Heyes's property, but he could well remember the last time he had viewed her work, and this time, he would not have to leave a cryptic little card. This time he would not be anonymous.

The home-made sign on the front door was turned to "open" and, rapping a short tattoo on the wood, he made his entrance. He could not have wished for a better reaction, as Minty, who was again sitting at the foot of the staircase, leapt up with a little "ooh!" of surprise and horror. Doom was writ large in her eyes as he formally introduced himself again and headed for her over-sized canvases.

Minty, her short hair standing on end where she had been running her fingers through it in despair, tottered behind him, offering staccato little phrases of explanation, only just restraining herself from throwing herself on his mercy, and begging him to be kind to her work this time.

Marcus maintained a stony silence, while inwardly smiling at the power he wielded. Should he be brutal, or should he take a more non-committal stance this time? He couldn't, as yet, make up his mind — her pieces *were* very striking, and displayed a wide palette. He'd leave it until later, he decided, and see what sort of mood he was in by the end of the day. He might even be nice — it really depended on how he felt when he had finished today's tour of inspection. After all, she had been kind to him the day before, conducting him to the village hall and introducing him to everyone.

Taking his leave of Minty with a curt handshake and just the merest hint of a smile, he turned his steps towards The Old School, to re-make the acquaintance of another artist whose work he had been scathing about. Minty watched his departure with confusion but little hope, and retook her seat at the foot of the stairs, sinking her head into her hands once more.

II

Sadie greeted his arrival much less timidly. Shaking him firmly by the hand (a little too firmly for Marcus's liking), she gave him a defiant smile and invited him into her studio. She then disappeared towards the other end of the house, leaving him to view her sculptures, ostensibly without an anxious creator in attendance, in reality because she felt, as she would have put it herself, "shit-scared".

In the kitchen, early in the day though it was, she poured a large slug of brandy into her inevitable cup of black coffee, and sat down at the table to wait, drumming her black fingernails restlessly on the table. All day yesterday, the old bastard had kept her and Minty in suspense, expecting him at any minute and dreading the moment he would arrive. Well, now he was actually here, albeit twenty-four hours after she had anticipated his arrival, he could trail round on his own. She would not give him the satisfaction of watching his reactions as he scrutinised each piece.

And she had left "Art Critic" in a fairly prominent place, and awaited his reaction with trepidation, mixed with just a morsel of glee.

She didn't have long to wait, as a howl of anger sounded from the studio. Scrambling to her feet she walked, her steps deliberately slow, towards the source of the fury, only to find Marcus in front of a totally different piece of sculpture, looking suspiciously innocent.

"Did I hear you call?" she enquired, sweet as saccharine.

"Er, yes," he admitted. "I, er, stubbed my toe on one of your, um, thought-provoking pieces of, um, statuary. I do hope I didn't disturb you in anything important."

"Not at all," admitted Sadie, and not at all taken in by his little act, either. He had seen "Art Critic" all right, and had identified himself as the inspiration. Well, let him put that in his pipe and smoke it. She would take the consequences, whatever they were, for, even without her little surprise, she was sure that the outcome would not have been in her favour. He could go to hell, as far as she was concerned. And if he slated her work again, she just might indulge in a little more retaliation this time, something a bit stronger and even more personal.

III

After a light lunch in The Inn on the Green (which had been rather slewed towards the liquid, for most of its content) Marcus made his way to the village hall once more. Settling himself in the middle of the front row of seats, he waited to be entertained.

At two thirty-two, only a couple of minutes late, Minty Wingfield-Heyes presented herself in the middle of the performance area and began to welcome the audience to the afternoon's entertainment. After a few sentences, however, she became aware of Marcus smiling pityingly at her, and began to gabble, rushing into her first introduction as if it were a race, and fled behind one of the screens, having peeped out Fiona Pargeter's name.

At this end of the hall, and slightly right of centre, stood a venerable piano at which Rollo Pargeter took his seat, spreading the sheets of his music across the music-stand in the order in which he would need to play it. His wife, Fiona, had no music — for this was unprofessional — and planted herself in the middle of the area, a smile of sweet anticipation on her face.

It all started so well — at least for the first six bars, when Rollo kindly pointed out in an audible whisper, that she was in the wrong key, and did she want him to transpose it? This did not bode well for the rest of her performance and, sure enough, as she ploughed through her three songs, her voice developed a strained quality, screeching more and more on the high notes, and straying sharp with nerves.

By the end of her final song she was wildly out of tune and barely scraping by, scrabbling at the high notes, as a drowning man clutches at a straw. Face red as a tomato, she had some guts though, for she bravely took her bow and did not bolt at the end of her performance. She walked off sedately, head held high to prevent the tears in her eyes from falling to a small scatter of applause from the more polite (or tone-deaf) members of the audience.

Minty briefly introduced Delia Jephcott in a high-pitched squeak, and the flautist came on carrying her music, stand and flute. After suitable arrangements with her music and the position of the stand, she raised her instrument to her lips and started to play.

It was quite a long piece, and all went well until about half-way through, when she turned her gaze upwards from her music, and locked eyes with Marcus Willoughby, leering knowingly from his throne-like position; exactly where a king would have sat if being entertained by his courtiers. A sudden bolt of fear shot through her and, although she tried desperately to control her breathing, she began to over-blow, making some of the notes jump an octave higher than they should have sounded.

Delia closed her eyes, for she knew the piece more or less by heart, to shut out the disturbing sight, and regained her composure about a quarter of the way before the piece ended. She had not covered herself with glory, she knew, but neither had she fled. She'd seen it out, admittedly with a bit of a wobble, but she had finished what she had intended to do, and now all she wanted was to get the hell out of that hall and run for home.

Having had such a minimal effect, Marcus's mood began to turn sulky. The liquid nature of the major part of his lunch was having its effect: he was beginning to get drowsy, and he was a nasty drunk, rather than the benevolent "I love everybody" kind.

Camilla Markland took to the stage next, unveiling her harp, which had stood, unnoticed and draped with a black silk sheet, to the rear of the left-hand side of the performance area. Rather unnerved by the two preceding performances, she took several deep breaths, before making herself comfortable and beginning to play.

A short way into her piece, her fingers fumbled and brought her to a halt. Gamely picking up where she had left off, she began again, but her hands were shaking now, the nerves really biting. When someone from the audience (recognised by those residents of Stoney Cross present as coming from a vulgar denizen of Steynham St Michael) called out, "Come back, Harpo Marx, all is forgiven!" Camilla's mind went completely blank. Her fingers froze, and, for a few ghastly seconds, there was a deathly silence. Into this silence, Camilla rose, and ran from the stage, sobbing, straight into the arms of her husband, Gregory, who escorted her tactfully from the venue. [Gee, this is going well, isn't it? Wish I'd been there!]

Lydia Culverwell, who was next, had to grit her teeth and summon up all her courage to approach the piano, wondering if, perhaps, she should have chosen something a little easier to play. But, too late now, she let loose her fingers in a welter of anxiety, starting reasonably, if not absolutely accurately, heard the few mistakes she had made, and thenceforth gave her audience a fair imitation of Les Dawson in exuberant musical mood.

Instead of sighs of emotion at the sad poignancy of Chopin's music, there were little giggles and sniggers and, by the time she had finished playing, gales of laughter buffeted her from the body of the hall. How humiliating! She knew it was only nerves, and that she was a fine pianist. How she would live this down, she had no idea.

At this point in the proceedings, Minty gabbled an announcement that they would take a half-hour break before the literary section of the performances, and would everyone like to adjourn to the refreshment tables, where tea, coffee, biscuits and cakes awaited them.

Marcus did not bother to comply with this suggestion, as he did not relish being bathed in scalding tea again and, leaving his jacket over the back of his chair, proceeded to The Inn to fortify his inner man with a few more drinks — he'd need them if he was

72

going to sit through any more of this. But needs must, if he was going to do a report on it for next week's programme, and, oh boy, was he now looking forward to that.

IV

Minty was already welcoming the audience to the second half of the programme when Marcus shambled down the aisle to the left of the seating and made his way, a little unsteadily, to his previous seat. Minty, originally relieved by his absence and hoping that he had had enough and gone home, immediately lost her way in her welcome, and peeped a clipped introduction to Christobel Templeton, their very own [amateur] poet.

Christobel crept, mouse-like, to take her place, dropping and picking up papers as she went. Why, oh why had she agreed to do this? Her husband, Jeremy, always encouraged her in her little efforts, and their cats, Byron and Longfellow, always attended to her contentedly when she read her verse to them. Now, for the first time, she doubted the quality of her poetry, and longed to be miles away and doing something completely different.

Nervously, she re-arranged her papers, cleared her throat, and began to read, in a somewhat tentative voice, "Nature's Bounty — by Christobel Templeton; that is to say — me."

Another clearing of the throat, then:

The sunbeams played for hours and hours,
Upon the hosts of lovely flowers
That grow upon this earth so fair,
To brighten up just everywhere.
In field and garden, park and pot
They always cheer us up a lot,
And leave their fragrance where they go
For all to smell and treasure so . . .

By the end of the fourth line, the audience had already become restive, and by the beginning of the eighth line, had begun a slow hand-clap, led, it was noticed, by those who didn't actually live in Stoney Cross — nobody resident in that village would have displayed such ill manners to dear, sweet, pretty Christobel. They would have applauded her efforts, and just said that she was so young, and merely needed time to grow as a poet.

Having no idea of this kindness, however, and now thoroughly unsettled by the censorious noise from the body of the hall, she halted, shuffled her papers again, mumbled a "thank you for your time", and slunk away through the emergency exit, thoroughly humiliated and embarrassed.

Marcus had joined in the slow hand-clap as he was feeling drowsy again, and agitated by the appalling standard of the offerings. He'd have liked to have had a refreshing little nap, but knew he would have to see this thing out first. Not only had he given his word [!], but he intended to shred every moment of this weekend when he got home and began to record his programme.

Hugo Westinghall was next to be thrown to the lions, but unexpectedly calmed the angry mob with the quality of his writing. Like his wife, he was a romantic novelist but, unlike her, he did not pepper his stories with sugary descriptions and cliché-ridden conversations. The audience calmed down under the restful tones of his voice, and really listened to the extract he read from his latest book. At the end of his oration, as he closed his book, there was a huge round of genuine applause, and a few of those present stamped their feet and whistled in appreciation. He left the stage with his head held high, greatly relieved that he had not received the treatment meted out to poor little Christobel.

Hugo's offering was followed by that of his wife, Felicity, but their styles varied considerably and she was, as yet, unpublished. As she droned on about strong hirsute hands creeping under bodices, and the sighs and moans of pleasure as a nipple was caressed here, an ear nibbled there, the audience became restive again.

Her many beads and bangles jangled and clattered over the flowing cotton of her long frock, as she began to tremble. Once or twice, her long dangling ear-rings caught in the material at her shoulders, and her reading was punctuated with the occasional "ouch" and "ow". That her voice was flat and monotonous did not help in any way, and soon, the hall was filled with boos and cat-calls.

Minty waited no longer, and thrust herself into the performance area, elbowing Felicity out of the way quite vigorously. Her appearance calmed things down, and she began to thank the audience for coming to their little entertainment, while silently thanking her lucky stars that they hadn't charged for it. They'd all want their money back, and there would be a hell of a row. At least it had been free, and they'd probably forget it all the more quickly as they hadn't had to put their hands in their pockets.

Finally, she apologised for the fact that there would be no dancing to end the programme, as their dancer, Serena Lyddiard had injured herself in practice, and she hoped that they would all wish her a speedy recovery. At this, Marcus pricked up his ears. This was the lady to whom he had not been introduced, and he was anxious to remedy the situation. He'd have to ask around in The Inn again, to see if he could pick up sufficient information to locate her geographically.

Rising from his seat and slipping on his jacket, he thought furiously as he headed, inevitably, back towards the public house.

CHAPTER
SEVEN

Sunday, 6th September — evening

I

The Inn was as busy as it had been since Friday evening; all the tables in the bar were occupied, and many more people were standing around in groups or at the bar. Peregrine and Tarquin were run off their feet, having failed, over the past few days, to secure any extra help. This was of no consequence, however, as it just meant that they would trouser more money for themselves.

Marcus sat at a table for two, alone, the second chair borrowed for use at another table. He had had some success with his prying and probing, and now sat, lost in a brown study, contemplating what he would say when he compiled his programme.

He was feeling particularly waspish and wickedly witty at the moment, but realised that he might have to lie low for a while after it was broadcast. In fact, he would have to keep a low profile *until* it was broadcast, not wanting any of that lot he had witnessed that afternoon, nor any of the artists, to beg him for a favourable review. He told it as he saw it, and would not compromise his honesty [*spite!*] for anyone.

He'd need to give them at least a couple of days to simmer down, maybe waiting until mid-week to make an appearance. Maybe not. And he'd better go into complete hiding on Friday afternoon for sure, for there would, no doubt, be many verbal "contracts" out on him after the programme, if he had anything to do with it. How could they expect anything else, after all those dreary pictures yesterday and that shameful shambles this afternoon?

II

At a table near the window sat that day's cast of performers, mostly untouched drinks before them, sunk in gloom at the way events had turned out. Christobel Templeton's eyes were red and puffy and she sat, like a disheartened mouse, with her husband's arm around her shoulder.

She was dreading the arrival of Friday afternoon, and didn't know how she would have the courage to face up to her radio-phonic humiliation. But even worse would be the days in between, with all her neighbours knowing what a fool she had been to think she could write poetry. She heaved a great heavy-hearted sigh, and absent-mindedly downed the double brandy that Jeremy had bought her to calm her nerves.

Felicity Westinghall was conspicuous by her absence. She had volunteered to look after the children this evening, an almost unheard-of occurrence. Hugo now

78

sat opposite Christobel, bathed in an aura of pride over his work. After all, he *was* published; Felicity was still working on achieving this level of acceptance. He had felt the odd pang of guilt at the difference in their readings' reception, but he wasn't going to let it burst his bubble. He'd "done his apprenticeship" years ago and was reaping the rewards for it now. Felicity would just have to work at achieving a more believable style.

Delia Jephcott, there with her partner Ashley in tow, was also looking suitably cowed by her experience that afternoon, but it was the presence of Marcus Willoughby in the village that was her biggest worry. What if Ashley found out? Whatever would he think of her? She'd always professed to having been absolutely single — had never wanted to have anything to do with marriage. Now she'd be caught out for the liar she was.

And she'd lied about her age when they'd moved here. Everyone knew she was a bit [*ha ha!*] older than Ashley, but not the extent of their age difference. This second thought worried her almost as much as the first one. Did people believe her, or were they silently mocking her? Well, if they didn't know now, they soon would, with that forked-tongued lizard around. What was she going to do? She'd just have to persuade Ashley to move away with her. She'd never be able to brazen out both of her little "secrets". And she just knew that she'd come down in the night and raid the fridge *and* the biscuit barrel, which would be followed by the inevitable consequences. She really would have to get a grip, or she'd have a third problem to face up to.

Ashley, totally oblivious to the turmoil taking place beside him, supped on, making the most of this visit to The Inn. It might not be the celebration everyone was hoping for, but he was just as willing to raise a glass or several to their failure. It made no difference to him, and maybe it would deflect Delia's attention from him for a couple of days, while she got over her humiliation.

Camilla Markland was similarly subdued, dealing with her inner turmoil by shovelling crisps into her mouth. Always slightly overweight, she envied her husband's metabolism — he could eat whatever he liked, and still stayed as thin as a rake. Oh, God! She stayed her hand, once again on its way to her mouth. What if he tells Greg? And another thought, much like Delia's: what if it gets about that I'm five years older than him? It might seem trivial to some people, but those people were usually men. Women were much more sensitive about that sort of thing, and it worried her terribly.

Fiona Pargeter and Lydia Culverwell were in an entirely different frame of mind, however. Having nothing to hide, and being absolutely blinkered about their lack of talent, they were head to head, in an indignant discussion about how their efforts would be reviewed. Usually the best of enemies, they had become the best of friends in adversity.

"It was definitely that piano," Lydia concluded on behalf of both of them. "Jangly old horror; I could hear it was out of tune when Rollo started playing your accompaniment. No wonder you had such trouble."

Fiona nodded her head in grateful agreement — it was much better than planting all the blame on her vocal chords. "And how could you be expected to play Chopin on what, in anyone's opinion, sounded like an old pub piano?" she sympathised. The truce would not, of course, last long, but for now, they were sticking together like . . . well, like a couple of very sticky things!

From an adjacent table, Sadie's strident voice made itself heard. "What was up with you this afternoon, Camilla? Couldn't see, because we'd forgotten to put in our turquoise-coloured contact lenses?"

Jerking her hand out of a packet of cheese-and-onion, and scattering crisps across the table, Camilla took a deep breath of fury and almost screamed across the pub, "You bitch! You said you wouldn't say anything if I didn't." Raking the bar at large with her disguised eyes, she continued, "She wears them too, you know! Only hers are blue. Those aren't her real eyes!" she concluded, slightly inaccurate in her fury.

"Oh, shut up and get a life, woman. I don't give a monkey's fart who knows about my lenses any more, but after this afternoon's little fiasco, I reckon you should wear your rose-tinted ones in future. Real life won't seem so painful through those." Sadie, feeling rather better than she had the day before, had decided it was someone else's turn in the barrel and, after several glasses of wine, had elected Camilla to the post.

III

That argument could have run and run, but there were very interesting noises coming from the bar where Marcus was trying, unsuccessfully, to obtain another drink.

"I really think you've had enough, sir." This was Tarquin, trying to be diplomatic, but doomed to make no headway, "And it *is* nearly closing time."

"I on'y wanna 'nother brandy." Marcus was definitely a bit the worse for wear, having started drinking at lunchtime. He had also made a trip back to The Inn at the interval, and returned straight after the disastrous performances had ended. He had eaten very little during this time, which had only exacerbated the speed of his inebriation.

"Why don't you just go home, sir? You must have had a very busy day; in fact, a very busy weekend." This was Peregrine, interjecting in support of his business partner.

"Don' wanna go home yet! Wan' 'nother drink."

Peregrine took the helm. "I'm sorry, sir, but we can't serve you."

"Why no'?"

"Because we think you've already had enough to drink, sir."

"How dare you!" Marcus sounded suddenly more sober as his dander rose. "How bloody dare you, you simpering, mincing couple of queers — you and your bleedin' poof-parlour gin-house. How bloody dare you! I wann' another brandy, and you *are* going to serve me, you soddin' arsebandits."

It took four strong male customers (*and* Sadie!) to remove him from the premises and send him on his way. But he wasn't done yet. He'd bloody show 'em! He'd show 'em all! For his was the kingdom, the power and the glory . . . With this religious theme rolling around in his mind, he turned towards the Church of St Peter and St Paul, with the idea that he had a bone to pick with "The Boss", and that this was definitely the right moment to do it.

IV

When the place was empty of customers and all the clearing away had been done, Peregrine and Tarquin sat down at one of the tables in the bar, between them a soda syphon, a bucket of ice and a bottle of Campari. "What an evening!" exclaimed Tarquin, the younger of the two men, sighing with relief that it was over.

"I couldn't agree more. And what a weekend! Still, we managed, in the end," agreed Peregrine.

They had, in fact, just finished enacting the story that Enid Blyton never got round to committing to paper — "Peregrine and Tarquin Pull it Off". "And what about that drunken old poseur, calling us a pair of poofs?" Peregrine added, taking a delicate sip of his Campari and soda and pursing his lips in a little moue of distaste.

"Exactly! And all the rest!" Tarquin was nodding his head in agreement. "Fancy calling us a pair of poofs," (here, he sighed, then continued), "when we're a brace of bi-s!"

Peregrine nearly choked on his drink in amusement.

V

Marcus staggered along School Lane, then turned unsteadily into Church Lane, his destination the Church of St Peter and St Paul. He had it in his befuddled mind that he was not receiving the respectful treatment he deserved from life, and, fuelled by an excess of alcohol and the resultant delusions of grandeur this state always induced in him, decided it was high time he had a word with someone about this — and he always went straight to the top.

There was no radio or television playing in The Vicarage, as Reverend and Mrs Ravenscastle were tidying up, in preparation for going up to bed. It was Adella who heard the noise first, the windows still being open. There seemed to be some sort of rumpus at the church, purposely (but foolishly) left unlocked by Benedict, in case should anyone wish to go in to pray.

Calling it to his notice, he stopped and listened. It sounded like someone shouting and, when there was a crash, as of something heavy being thrown or pushed over, Benedict headed for the door. "I don't know what's going on over there, but it sounds like I'd better take a look," he called over his shoulder. "I was going to go over in a few minutes and lock up for the night anyway."

"Do be careful, Benedict, dear. You don't know who's in there or what they're doing. There could be a whole mob of them, for all you know."

"It sounded like one person to me, and remember, I put my faith in the Lord for my protection." So saying,

84

he closed the door and hastened towards the porch of the church.

Inside, he found an inebriated Marcus Willoughby, standing by an overturned pew and shaking his fist heavenwards. "If you really *do* exist, you're a right bastard. You *know* I'm important, yet you le' me be *humiliated* like this," he roared, and carried on in this vein until Benedict laid a gentle hand on his left shoulder.

"Steady, old man!" he soothed, moving round so that he was face to face with Marcus. "I don't know what all this fuss is about, but why don't you just slip off home to bed; sleep it off, and come and see me in the morning if you'd like to talk about it." It cost him a lot to be so solicitous to the man who had torn his family apart, but his respect for the position he held deemed it necessary.

"Soddin' fraud!" Marcus bellowed.

"That's a bit strong, old chap. I'm just offering you pastoral care."

"No' you, 'im — your bleedin' God. 'E doesn't ez, ez, ez . . . ezzist. A' my life 'e's 'ad it in for me, an' I jus' wanna bi' of a break. Even tho' 'e do'n' ezzist." Marcus's speech had deteriorated again as his rage settled a little. "An' ge' your 'ands off me, you no goo' God-botherer-erer," he continued firmly, losing his way on the last word.

Benedict put an arm across Marcus's shoulder and began to guide him, slowly but surely, towards the door. The only light in the church coming from the votive lamp, it was not until he had almost reached the porch

85

that he saw the face of his wife, a distressed expression on her face, peering in at them. Adella shrank away from them as they exited, and her husband pointed Marcus in the general direction of his own home. They watched as he tottered away, still mumbling and complaining under his breath. He'd get 'em all! He was going home to record his programme, and he'd rip them to ribbons. Tear them to shreds. They'd treat him with a proper respect in future. He'd tell the whole world what a bunch of bitchy, treacherous and talentless nobodies they were, *then* they'd be sorry, and he'd be top dog again. His programme would wipe out their pathetic little Festival, or he was a Dutchman.

Sharpening his mental claws, an evil smile spread slowly up his face, finally reaching his eyes. He would assassinate them, each and every one, and expose their pathetic little secrets. He'd leave them raw and begging for mercy, by the time he'd finished with them. And then, he thought, it might just be time to move on — possibly to the Caribbean, he quite fancied that. Maybe coming to Stoney Cross hadn't been such a good idea after all . . .

CHAPTER
EIGHT

Monday, 7th September — early hours

I

It was nearly two o'clock when Adella Ravenscastle was woken by her husband trying to creep upstairs to join her in bed. "Where on earth have you been at this time, Benedict?"

"Sorry, my love. I couldn't contemplate sleep after that thing with Willoughby, so I went for a bit of a walk to calm my temper, then I went and prayed for a while."

"What about?" asked Adella, knowing she shouldn't ask.

"For forgiveness for him for what happened tonight, and for remorse and forgiveness for what he has done to our family. I also prayed for understanding for myself, and that I should be given the strength to really forgive him for his awful sin of taking a life."

"Oh, Benedict, I don't think I can stand it: him living here in our parish, and having to see him, bump into him when I least expect it. I don't know if I can keep my nerve. I don't know even if I can keep my temper."

"God will give you the strength, my dear. And don't forget, we aren't the only ones suffering due to his presence. Squirrel was just beginning to come to terms with Bubble's loss — yes, I know it was only a dog, but he was family to her — and now *he's* turned up and re-opened the wound. I haven't seen her since she baptised him in tea," he concluded, quite pleased at his little clerical joke. If it was a weak one, he did not care. So had the tea been. "Let's just sleep on it for now, and I'll go round to see Squirrel tomorrow, see how she is."

He fell, immediately, into a deep sleep as his head touched the pillow, but Adella continued muttering to herself, finally finishing her thoughts with, Well, if no one else is going to do anything about it, I am — and I know just what! I can do nothing to bring back our darling Maria, but there's something I *can* fix. I just need to give it a little thought.

Thoroughly awake by now, her mind busy with her plan, she got out of bed, slipped on a light coat, and some shoes, and, taking only a moment to scribble a note should Benedict wake and find her gone, left the house. Although nothing short of a bomb would usually wake Benedict, she took this precaution out of courtesy and, apart from anything else, she needed some air. She was a woman on a mission, and would not let the lateness of the hour delay her plan.

Many of Stoney Cross' resident performers were unable to sleep after the debacle of their presentations that day, and none of the artists was quite at ease, either. There were far too many possibilities concerning what would happen next, and quite a few people took to their cars, or to the lanes for a walk. Although none of them actually had a physical encounter with one another, there were many figures flitting about, mostly lost in thought, or seething with anger. May God have mercy on Marcus when he finally showed his face — he would need it!

II

Two of those who stayed put were Delia Jephcott and Camilla Markland.

In Starlings' Nest, Delia was screwing herself up to tell Ashley that she had been married to Marcus for a brief while, over twenty years ago. She was dreading his reaction, and terrified that she might lose her toy-boy; for she did love him, and hoped he loved her enough to forgive this little oversight on her part, about her past. He, after all, would have been only about seven or eight years old at the time . . . though that would highlight their age difference in his mind. God forbid — he might even leave her!

As calmly as she could, her voice trembling only a little, she managed to speak the awful words and reveal the details of her darkest secret. As she finished, she was about to throw herself on Ashley's mercy, when he suddenly shouted with laughter, and caught her up in a totally unexpected hug. "You silly mare!" he declared. "I don't care what you did before you met me, because that's all in the past, and none of us can change the past. All that matters is now; and "now" means you and me. Give us a kiss, dopey."

When she had disentangled herself, Delia examined his expression minutely. "You really don't mind?"

"More than that, I really don't *care*. What's the use of getting all bent out of shape by things we can't change?"

"Ashley Rushton, you are the best man in the world, and I'm so glad we're together." Delia's voice was quivering with emotion again, and un-spilled tears shone in her eyes.

"Come here, you silly old thing," he almost crooned, gathering her into his arms again.

"And not so much of the 'old'," she admonished him, her voice muffled by his shoulder, where she had buried her face in relief. "Look, I know it's late, but I'm going to go for a little stroll. I'm just so relieved that everything is out in the open, and you're not packing your suitcase."

"Silly, silly Delia! Did you really think I was so shallow?"

"Well, I do nag you a bit, but no, darling, it's just . . ." Her voice trailed into silence. She smiled at him with relief and went to get that fresh air she needed.

III

Camilla Markland was not so lucky with her husband Gregory's reaction to her "little confession".

"You did *what?*," he shouted in disbelief.

90

"It was after that concert in Carsfold last year. I was absolutely smashed, what with nerves, champagne and adrenalin. I've never been so drunk, Greg, and he took advantage of my condition."

"Yeah, I'll bet he did. With you probably offering it to him on a plate, how could he possibly refuse?"

"It wasn't like that!" she protested.

"What was it like, then? Do you want to tell me, or would you rather I imagined it?"

"Greg! I was absolutely off my face. I barely remember it! I just remember waking up the next day, realising what I'd done, and feeling as if my life was over."

"You tart! You whore! And with that shrivelled, pompous old . . ." Greg Markland spluttered himself to a verbal standstill in his rage.

"I've said I'm sorry, and I'm still mortified about it. Please, please don't be too hard on me. I've been in hell ever since. And now he's moved to the same bloody village, I knew it'd come out sooner or later, and I wanted to tell you first, before you heard it from him, or from someone else."

"Shut up, shut up, shut up! You bloody slut! I'm going out, and I don't know whether I'll be coming back. And if I do, it'll just be to collect my stuff when I've found somewhere to stay."

"Greg, please don't leave me. I'll do anything — anything."

"Oh, I know you will, and you've just told me all about it. That's us finished, as far as I'm concerned!" and he bolted from the room, leaving Camilla slumped on the sofa, wailing and sobbing at the catastrophe that had overtaken her.

IV

Stoney Cross could take on a darker air by night. When The Inn on the Green had locked its door and closed for another day, the revellers dispersed, laughing and shouting, towards their own homes, the contrasting almost-silence had an unnerving quality about it. Many everyday objects that tell us where we are in time, such as satellite dishes, were lost in shadows. The street lighting was dim, as if it were still produced by gas, and the narrow roads and old buildings were also deceptive as to exactly when "now" was — it could have been any time within the last hundred and fifty years or so. To a drunken mind, it was confusing and intimidating.

Wisps and tendrils of mist from the nearby river, the Little Darle, floated and crept like questing fingers through the streets and gardens, adding an other-worldliness to the atmosphere. The village itself raged at Marcus, enveloping him in sudden foggy clouds that temporarily blinded him, making him stumble on unseen obstacles, and lose his way to such an extent that, at one point, he found himself in the middle of the road. He had to execute a nifty side-step to avoid an oncoming vehicle, which was travelling, fortunately for him, very slowly in the prevailing weather conditions, and swore under his breath as it moved invisibly away. The village was showing its flip-side — the side that remembered violence, deprivation, hunger and great hardship, and it teased Marcus's imagination, quickening his pace, and making his heart beat a little faster as he approached the safety of his new home.

Still feeling bloody-minded, his first action, after sitting down at his desk, was to pour himself a large brandy, pull the phone toward him, extract a small scrap of paper from his pocket, and punch in a number with rather more vigour than was necessary. Without giving the recipient of the call the chance to speak, he intoned, "Jenny! You can't hide away any more. I told you the last time. I've found you! I've *really* found you now! And our daughter will want to visit you when she returns. Isn't that just lovely and cosy, after all this time? We can start being a proper family. Won't that be nice?"

But there was only the dialling tone, as he got to the end of his torturing reminder. Replacing the receiver, he rubbed his hands together in squiffy glee, and pulled his mini-recorder towards him to go through his earlier oral notes, with a view to getting his next programme polished off before he went to bed. The memories of his more outrageous behaviour were already distant and faint, more like phantoms. He felt like the king of the world, about to wield his power and feeling so "goo-ooo-ood".

He was well into his stride when, unbeknown to him, a car crawled along the High Street through the mist, its engine noise muffled by the weather conditions. A car with no lights, and making as little noise as possible, given the circumstances, finally coasting as it reached the drive of The Old Barn. It could have been the car of any of the people he had upset that weekend, that day, that evening, but the driver was unidentifiable in the gloom of the vehicle's interior, the dim street-lighting, and the obscuring quality of the mist.

An entirely anonymous figure, it exited the vehicle, closing the driver's door as quietly as possible, and made its way round towards the side of the property, where a light shone out on to the lawn from a pair of French windows, slightly ajar to let the heat of the day out and the cool of the night in.

So engrossed was he in his mischief-making recording — he was now working straight on to the computer program — that he had no notion that someone had entered the room, walking quietly in bare feet. He was oblivious to the fact that that someone now stood behind him, arms raised, with something stretching between, and wound around, clenched fists.

Yes, Stoney Cross was angry tonight, and the cause of that anger would soon suffer punishment . . .

CHAPTER
NINE

Monday, 7th September — morning

The Festival, after all the planning, hopes, ambitions and fears, had arrived, had ground its way to its ghastly conclusion, and now it only remained for the clearing-up to be done.

The "usual suspects" were at the village hall, bagging up Styrofoam cups, and biscuit and crisp packets, clearing away the tables, chairs and screens, and leaving the artwork in little piles, to be collected by their creators sometime that day.

Serena, too, was there, having no trouble with transport, as her car was an automatic and could be driven with one foot, if necessary. She sat in state, on a chair near the piano, in what had been the performance area, her left leg propped up on another chair for support.

Most of those present worked with relief that the whole experience was over and done with, but a few sat on stray chairs, apparently lost in a world of their own. Camilla Markland, usually so full of herself and her own opinions, was slumped in a chair at the rear of the hall near the doors, tears rolling down her face, her slightly beaky nose red and raw. To anyone who approached to see what was wrong, she gave a slight shake of the head, and turned away for a moment. She had not wanted to sit alone in her empty house, waiting for the sounds that Greg would never again make. So steeped in unhappiness was she that she had no hopes for his return, and contemplated a bleak and lonely future.

At the other end of the hall Adella Ravenscastle sat, reaching down now and again to pet her Dachshund, Satan. On her face was an enigmatic smile. She let it rest there for the remainder of her time in the hall.

Lydia, Fiona, Sadie, Minty, Delia, and Ashley worked with a will, while conducting a patchy and disjointed conversation. When Fiona dropped a glass sugar bowl with a resounding tinkle, Rollo, who was passing the piano at the time, crashed a chord of E min dim7 with both hands, followed by a two-octave D min, and finishing the flourish with a basement D, an octave below bottom D. This caused some amusement from those present, and even raised a smile from Camilla. Adella, however, carried on staring into the distance, still smiling her tiny smile, hugging her secret to herself like a child with a teddy bear.

Christobel was not present, having begged her husband, Jeremy, to stay home with her for support, and not go to the grand clear-up, for fear he would return with tales of derogatory comments about her doggerel. That she would never write poetry again, she was absolutely sure; and she would not even be able to show her face in Stoney Cross for quite a while. She anticipated her self-imposed isolation with a sort of grim pleasure — a meting out of her own punishment, while avoiding all the back-biting and bitchery of other people in the immediate future.

Also lending a helping hand were Felicity and Hugo Westinghall, their children, inevitably, throwing bread at the ducks on the pond along with the Pargeter children. Ducks that were now overflowing with largesse, and probably bruises, for the bread was always stale and sometimes rock-hard. A few of the other exhibiting artists were also part of the team, having been shamed into helping when they arrived to collect their pictures.

Sadie and Minty were unexpected attendees, as they had shown their works at home. Their motives, however, were rooted in sheer nosiness — the need to know how other participants were feeling, so that they could compare this with their own reactions.

At eleven o'clock or thereabouts, the two of them slipped off to a bench on the village green so that Sadie could have a cigarette or two, and they could compare notes. Taking their seats on the bench furthest from the pond and its coterie of eavesdropping little ears, they sat just the other side of the hedge that divided Sadie's home from the green. Minty made the opening bid.

"I thought I was going to wet myself again, this time with fear," she admitted, twisting her hands together in this remembered anguish.

"That would have gone down well," Sadie replied, with the ghost of a chuckle.

"Well, he's got such cold eyes, and he never said a word about my stuff. I dread to think what he's going to say about it on the programme," Minty continued, running one hand through her short hair — a habit she had when unnerved. "But what about you? Did he see that *thing*?"

"He did indeed see it."

"And what did he say? Was he really angry? Did he make a scene and have a go at you?"

"Nothing at all like that," Sadie recounted, with a slight upturn of her mouth. "I was in the kitchen when there was this almighty yell. I just knew he'd seen it, and went rushing in, not having a clue what I was going to say in my own defence. And he said nothing at all about *it*. He pretended he'd stubbed his toe on another of my lumps of stone, and left shortly afterwards. But I'll tell you something: I had an anonymous offer on it through the letter-box, for twice what I had it priced up at."

"Surely, not from him?" Minty was wide-eyed with surprise and speculation.

"I think so. Obviously it wasn't signed, and I don't know his handwriting or his home phone-number, but I know it in my bones."

"But why would he want it?" Minty was now puzzled, not being very good at devious motives.

"For one of two reasons," Sadie began, in explanation. "Either he wanted to take a sledge hammer to it and destroy it, or he was more twisted than that. Perhaps he was going to hide it away. Maybe, for all his previous criticism, he realised I have real talent, and proposed to display it when I'm well known. Then it would become a delightful joke for him, even if the joke was *on* him, because it would make him seem like an old friend who had colluded in the piece."

"God, Sadie, however do you think of these things?" Minty was definitely impressed.

"I expect I've got a streak of devilish cunning running right through me," answered her friend, tossing aside her cigarette butt and beginning to rise. "Come on, you! There's more work to be done before we can go to The Inn and reap our just rewards."

Tuesday, 8th — Thursday, 10th September

It did not take long for a nine-days'-wonder to turn into a two-or three-days'-wonder, and life in Stoney Cross returned to its previously uninterrupted and peaceful existence. A few incidents, however, were worthy of note: changes wrought by Marcus moving to the village, and his air of "slumming it" at the Festival.

Felicity Westinghall had signed up for a creative writing course in Market Darley, determined to "up her game" to a standard where she could realistically compete with Hugo.

Lydia Culverwell had determined never to perform in public again, explaining her decision in one word — nerves. It was a face-saver, and was, in part, true. She could play well; was not a bad pianist, but fell to pieces before an audience. That she could play competently at home was one thing, but in front of others, on an alien instrument, her fingers became like two bunches of bananas, and there was nothing at all she could do about it.

The eyes of Camilla Markland were now appearing naked in public. For everyday life, now that her secret was out, she shunned her once-beloved coloured contact lenses, reserving them only for concerts and other public performances. In her post-confessional state of misery, she couldn't have worn them anyway, she wept so much. Nobody in Stoney Cross was fooled any more, so what was the point? That she received a glimmer of respect for this, she would have been surprised to discover, and would later wonder why she had been so vain in the past.

She had had a few agonisingly miserable days on her own. Days drowned in tears of grief and loss, then on Thursday evening, she had been startled to hear a key in the door, and overcome with joy to see Greg come through the front door. The thought that he might have come back just to collect some possessions never entered her mind, and she threw herself at him, wrapping her arms round him and crying (again) with relief. And she was lucky in her assumption because, having thought long and hard, he had decided, for now, that one small slip (stupid and faithless though it was), should not break up a marriage that had survived so long without any other such damaging incidents. Their reunion was both passionate and tender, and they must be left to enjoy it in privacy.

Serena Lyddiard still spent most of her time at home. One leg elevated, she sat in her armchair while

100

others telephoned or visited, keeping her up to date with everything that she had missed at the Festival, and any other village tittle-tattle that they thought would interest her, including the fact that Marcus seemed to have gone to ground. On Thursday afternoon, she ventured a tentative walk into the village, with just a crepe bandage and a walking stick for support, looking forward to her return to a more sociable life, and one of the tea-shop's excellent coffee éclairs (made on the premises, of course).

At The Vicarage, Adella Ravenscastle had confounded her husband by being rather distant and secretive, occasionally humming quietly, and going about her daily chores with a new briskness. She had been thrown back into the maws of an old grief at Marcus's arrival, and yet, here she was, whizzing around with a duster and looking, if not radiant, then at least much more at peace. Her husband asked nothing, preferring to remain in ignorance if his wife was no longer tearful and full of anger.

Of Squirrel, there had been no sign since the tea-throwing incident, and she and her little Yorkie were beginning to be missed. With this in mind, the vicar walked across to her cottage in Church Lane after saying a lone evensong. The little house was in darkness, and at first there was no answer to his knock. At his second knock, however, a muffled "wuff" was just audible and, knowing that there was a key below the heavy doormat, he retrieved it and let himself in.

The house smelled stale and unaired, a foul undertone bringing Squeak to the fore of his mind, but downstairs there was no sign of life. The living room was undusted and untidy, overcrowded with ornaments, recent purchases from car-boot sales piled on chairs and under the table. The kitchen was a complete mess, with dirty crockery in the sink and on the kitchen table, and flies buzzed around Squeak's empty food bowls. Venturing upstairs, he followed the faint doggy noises and found Squirrel in her bed, her little dog at the foot of it, both of them looking weak and forlorn.

Instantly taking in the situation, he carried the feather-light dog down to the kitchen, where he opened a tin of dog food and filled the water bowl, opening the back door as he did so, with the twin intentions of letting in some fresh air and letting out the flies, along with the foul smell from the dog's "accidents of necessity". Squeak had obviously not had access to the garden for some time — his nose had confirmed this when he had first opened the front door.

He then proceeded to open a tin of soup he found in a wall cupboard and put it on to the hob to heat, while he made a pot of tea. There was no edible bread to be found, but he felt that was not of too much importance, as Squirrel had obviously not eaten for some time, and would need to go gently with her stomach at first, so as not to overload it.

Taking these offerings upstairs, he fed the old lady, then persuaded her to go to the bathroom for a long-overdue cleanup, finding fresh sheets in a chest at the foot of the old brass bed and changing them before her return. It was an hour later when he left to go home, taking the soiled linen with him and promising

102

that he would set up a rota of visitors, both for company and household chores. Her shopping he would see to himself, taking Squeak with him for a little much-needed exercise and an opportunity to conduct some business of his own.

These arrangements made, he returned to The Vicarage, seething with fury that the mere presence of Willoughby in the village could have had such catastrophic effects on one of his flock. And he, personally, would find it hard to forgive him for what had happened in the past, and the blasphemous things he had said in God's house just a few days ago. For once, prayer did not seem to be doing any good.

Christobel Templeton had taken a surprisingly short time to recover from her public humiliation and the realisation that she was no poet. She had turned, instead, to the planning of a gory murder story, in which a thinly-disguised Marcus Willoughby was the victim, dying horribly, slowly, and in agony. Not only was it therapeutic, but it dispelled her embarrassment and anger, and gave her something to do. A distraction from memories, and a view to the future.

But she was soon to lose interest in this, as the humiliation flooded back, and plunged her, once more, into despair. If she was no poet, then she was probably no author either, and her life felt empty and pointless again, the initial adrenalin rush of wreaking her revenge seeping away, like rainwater into the ground.

Minty had adopted the same attitude as Sadie after a long chat on the telephone and, knowing that her work was good, had agreed to join Sadie to see if they could get a joint display in Market Darley, with the help of an old friend who had rather a large van. That way, others would get to see their work, and could judge it for themselves.

Sadie had been highly amused by the contact lens incident and had bought herself a new pair. She now sported one vivid blue and one rich chocolate-brown lens, to the consternation of everyone who encountered her, and was delighted with the effect she was having on people she knew. She liked this look, and would have some fun swapping them around — one day, right eye brown, the next, left eye brown. What a great effect she would have with strangers and viewers of her sculptures. They'd remember her, and no mistake.

Late Thursday evening, after closing, Summer Leighton parked at The Inn on the Green and knocked vigorously at the door. Inside, Peregrine and Tarquin, both a little grumpy at the slackening of trade after the rush over the Festival weekend, had fallen to discussing the offensive remarks passed by their customers on the local radio celebrity since his last visit to The Inn, and re-visiting his offensive remarks about them.

Although they were all too aware of homophobia, much of it had disappeared over the last few years, leaving more of a laissez-faire attitude. People might still think it, but, especially around here, they didn't say anything, which was fine. Those who did were usually telling a joke, or making a point about different lifestyles. Marcus's tirade had been different, however. He had been all "hail fellow, well met" until they had refused to serve him, then he had shown his true colours. And they had not been pretty, but full of hatred, bigotry and spite.

The conversation was cut off so abruptly by the knock at the door that the sudden silence could have been the result of a radio being turned off. They were aware that Summer would be arriving that night as she had booked a room that morning, but they had expected her a little earlier than this. They also knew of her relationship to Marcus Willoughby (that homophobic bastard!), but didn't want to lose custom by offending one of their customers, especially one who had made a booking, and would more than likely patronise their establishment for refreshments during her stay.

As they mounted the stairs to the letting rooms, Peregrine went in front of her to show the way, Tarquin behind, making a face and poking his tongue out at Peregrine, because he had been left to carry her bag, and it weighed a ton. Maybe Willoughby was building an extension, and Summer had offered to bring the bricks, he thought sarcastically, as he felt the strain on his shoulder muscles.

"You haven't seen anything of my father, Mr Willoughby, have you?" she asked, sounding just a little uncomfortable with using "my father" in relation to Marcus.

"He hasn't been in since Sunday night, Ms Leighton," answered Peregrine, who addressed all women as Ms these days unless told otherwise, lest he cause offence.

"What, not at all? Not even out and about in the village?"

"Sorry, love." Tarquin was not so politically correct. "I'm afraid he was a teensy bit annoyed when he left us, so maybe he's sent us to Coventry."

I'll walk up and see him tomorrow, Summer decided, scratching her head and thinking. "I'm going to have a long lie-in in the morning," she decided, out loud, "then sometime late-afternoon-ish, I'll head on up there. It's funny, you know, I haven't had a reply to my telephone calls, my e-mails or my texts. He must be very busy."

Settling himself on the bed in her room rather presumptuously, Tarquin gave her a brief account of what he knew concerning the events of last weekend, but did it in such a way that the seriousness of it all was not emphasised, giving the impression that it was all a rather jolly collection of misunderstandings, and just rather bad luck. She was not, therefore, alarmed at his tale, and settled down to unpack, leaving her plan to visit The Old Barn late tomorrow afternoon unrevised.

In fact, nobody had seen Marcus since Sunday, when he returned home from The Inn. Nobody at all — except one!

CHAPTER
TEN

Friday, 11th September — afternoon

I

Every radio except one was tuned to Radio Carsfold well before three o'clock that Friday. Those who had participated in the Festival waited in dread; those who hadn't, in high anticipation of as good a dose of *Schadenfreude* as they were likely to get for some time to come. One radio stayed, of necessity, silent.

After the opening jingle came the programme announcement. "And now for our weekly dose of the arts, with our very own Village Culture Vulture, Mr Marcus Willoughby." There was a miniscule pause, and Marcus's unmistakeably haughty voice began to intone.

"Now, last week I told you about an Arts Festival that was going to take place in Stoney Cross on the fifth and sixth of this month. I want to offer my apologies at the very beginning of the programme to any of you who decided to attend . . ." Hackles were already beginning to rise in Stoney Cross.

"For any of you who did *not* attend the art exhibition in the village hall, let me tell you, you were the lucky ones." Marcus's voice was already sounding just a little off-kilter, not quite the precise enunciation they were used to. As Peregrine remarked to Tarquin, "Maybe he had "the drink taken"."

"All I can say about it was that all the visual exhibits were unspeakably amateurish. They were, each and every one of them, badly executed, with no eye for proportion, perspective or colour . . ." In his cubicle at the radio station, his producer sighed, and wondered why they had ever taken a chance on this man. They knew he was controversial from his arts reports in the local paper. Malice of this level, they had not expected. Still, he'd not checked the contents beforehand, and would have to continue with the broadcast now. It didn't matter what he did; he would be damned either way.

". . . and as for the Artists Trail — oh my goodness, I wished I'd stayed at home and stuck pins in my eyes. At the home of Ms Sadie Palister, I thought there had been a recent delivery from the quarry, until I realised that what I was looking at were her finished works. Need I say more?

"Just before that visit, I had called on Ms Araminta Wingfield-Heyes who imagines herself an abstract artist. Well, abstract her works may be, but art, they certainly are not. Had they been smaller, they would have been less painful on the eye and one's sensitivities, and I respectfully [!] suggest that she paints miniatures in the future, and hangs them face to the wall.

"I turn now to the performances in the village hall on Sunday last, an experience, the likes of which I hope

108

never to have the misfortune to repeat. The 'show' (listeners could hear the inverted commas) was opened by Ms Lydia Culverwell on the piano. I don't know who told her she could play, but, I for one, have never heard such a badly fingered cacophony. To paraphrase the words of one of our late, great comedians, she might possibly have been playing all the right notes, but definitely, without a shadow of a doubt, not in the right order. And if I may add to that, not in the right village, for I wished her anywhere but where I was."

As the programme continued, so the clarity of Marcus's speech deteriorated, his next little poisoned needle preceded by a discreetly muffled hiccough. "The next offering was a flute recital, given by Ms Delia Jephcott, and it would have been better if she'd tackled the "Unfinished", because she screeched through a portion of her piece, then fled from the stage," he lied cattily, "And that was the best bit, because we didn't have to suffer any more of her appalling playing . . ."

As he droned on, tempers were rising, fists clenching and teeth grinding in Stoney Cross. Everyone had worked so hard for their Festival, and here was this *incomer*, this *nobody*, stamping all over their efforts and trampling on their dreams, without a thought for their feelings. Hostile thoughts were forming, as were even wilder ones of revenge, but still the listeners did not switch off — mesmerised by the now-familiar voice, unable to disengage themselves from its spite.

". . . Pargeter, who calls herself a singer. Well, let me tell you, dear listeners, I've heard better from an East End pub on a Saturday night after closing time. This

was definitely an act of piracy — death on the high Cs."
As he concluded these acid remarks, his voice rose in
pitch and volume, beginning to sound a little
demented.

Calming down slightly, his contumely continued.
"Ms Camilla Markland, a lovely girl I have had the
pleasure of meeting before," he drawled, his voice now
with a lascivious tone, "and would not mind meeting
again . . . Anyway, I digress!" Here, he seemed to pull
himself together, and got back to the assassination in
hand. "This delightful lady is unfortunately deluded,
believing as she does, that she has mastered her chosen
instrument: the harp. I have a feeling that she was cured
of her delusion in that village hall, for she left, sobbing,
as if enlightenment had indeed struck.

"Now, moving on the literary section of the
performances . . ." Christobel Templeton finally summoned up the strength, not to turn off the little radio,
but to hurl it to the floor and stamp on it, like a child
throwing a tantrum. "I can't stand any more," she
shouted. "Doesn't he think I was humiliated enough on
the day?"

"I agree," her husband said, putting his arms around
her. "It's not as if you're a professional. It was done
with a good heart, and I would have thought that he'd
have had the common sense to see that. He's just using
the Festival to further his reputation as "fearless and
controversial", as he no doubt believes it to be. Forget
it and come and have a nice cup of tea." Jeremy was
doing his level best to be a "knight in shining armour".
He knew he should have persuaded her against reading

her verse, but she had been so excited at the prospect, and now look where it had got them. Thank God she had lost her nerve, and managed to avoid the cutting words Marcus would have produced, had he heard her entire offering.

". . . unacceptable and unbearable twaddle. The sort of doggerel that sounded as if it had been written by a seven-year-old." Other radios had not been destroyed, and continued to broadcast his contumely. "Now, after Ms Templeton came the only passable few minutes of the whole shebang. Hugo, Hugo West . . . West, Westinghall — that's the chap — well, he, at least, is a published author and, although I don't like the whole romantic novel thing — the genre — Hugo's effort wasn't too shabby. But then we had his — hic! — wife, Felic-ic-icity." Marcus was beginning to disintegrate before his listeners' very ears, and a lot of head-scratching, actual and metaphorical, was being carried out in Stoney Cross, and at the radio station.

"The whole thing was slushy, sloppy, ungram . . . ungrammat-at-at-ical, and drowning in a sea of unnec-ecessay wor's. Prob'ly the worst load of unimagin-aginative an' banal drivel I've heard for man', for man', — for many — for ages." His voice was running down like a musical box, when the radio broadcast a yell of surprising volume, there was a short period of grunting and scuffling, and then, silence.

After two minutes, actually a very long time in broadcasting, the producer's voice cut in to apologise for this loss of transmission, and offered them, in the meantime some music, while the radio station sorted out its "little technical problem".

As others were left wondering what on earth this meant, Summer, who had been listening in the bar of The Inn on the Green, rushed outside, pounded up School Lane and into the High Street in the direction of The Old Barn. She knew nothing about radiophonic technical problems, but she did know that she had been unable to contact her father for days, by any means that she had tried, and that final few seconds of the broadcast had sent her into a panic. Something dreadful had happened, she was sure, and she wouldn't be calmed until she had seen him.

She saw him, all right.

II

In the police headquarters in Market Darley, DI Harry Falconer was in a brown study of his own, contemplating the outcome of a recent case in the village of Castle Farthing, and the unsatisfactory conclusion that it had reached. He should have been more astute — should never have allowed the possibility of such a thing happening.[1]

He raised his chocolate-brown eyes to the ceiling and frowned at the memory, as the phone on his desk began to trill its urgent summons. Shaking his head to summon his mind back to the present, he lifted the receiver and listened. "Oh, not another one, surely? . . .

---

[1] See *Death of an Old Git*: The Falconer Files book 1.

Where, this time? . . . Good God, not in another one of those God-forsaken villages? Who, this time?" There was a longer pause as he listened to the explanation. "In the middle of a radio programme? I don't believe it! Death on the air, as I live and breathe! Who will I take? . . . Oh, no, not again! This cannot be happening! OK, OK. Yes, I'll just give him a shout."

Falconer ran his immaculately manicured fingers through his short dark hair, and expostulated, "This area gets more like . . . *Midwinter Murders* every day. Nothing happens for years, then two murder investigations come along at once. And so it looks like I've got the part of Inspector . . . *Carnaby*." The incident at Castle Farthing had only just been wrapped up, and here they were again, with another corpse on their hands. Checking his attire with a quick glance down, he decided that he would have to go home and change into something less expensive, opened the office door, and bellowed, "Carmichael! I have need (he groaned inwardly) of your company."

A voice called, "Coming!" and, a minute and a half later, a uniformed policeman, nigh on six-and-a-half feet in height, ducked slightly to enter the room. "You called, sir?" asked this apparition, hair sticking out at all angles, uniform jacket buttoned askew, and a pen behind one ear.

"I did indeed, Carmichael. My usual sergeant is currently on paternity leave." Falconer almost spat out the last two words, disgusted at how namby-pamby the world had become since he was a child, and continued, "and Steve Milligan is on sick leave for stress, the selfish sod, probably hoping for early retirement on medical grounds; so you're going to have to go home and get changed. You're going to be my Acting DS on another murder case."

"Another one, sir?" Carmichael's face registered a mixture of delight and disbelief. How could he get this lucky?

"Your ears did not deceive you. Now, get off home, and try to dress like a human being — and preferably *not* an American one. I don't want to be seen in public with someone who looks like a Hank or a Zeke. Now, jump to it, and I'll pick you up from your place." Looking at Carmichael's shirt collar, stained with dirty finger marks, he sighed and said, "Stick your tongue out for me." Carmichael did so, without question, and sure enough, it was stained purple. He'd been sucking the wrong end of his ballpoint pen. Again!

Back at his home, a nineteen-fifties detached house with a clinical and minimalist interior, Falconer carefully hung up his light linen suit on the wardrobe door, deciding that he needed something just a little warmer (and cheaper!) for his trip into "banjo country", as he thought of it. He would take the linen suit in for pressing on the way to Stoney Cross, so that it was presentable the next time he wanted to wear it. An ex-army man, it was a job he should have undertaken himself, but life was too short and his working hours too long. He liked his free time to be just that — free.

Starting the engine in his Boxster once more, he headed off in the direction of Carmichael's home in

Victoria Terrace. His Acting DS lived in a rather ramshackle extension at the back of his family's terraced house, the latter recognisable by the number of derelict and abandoned vehicles in its front garden. Carmichael's "private residence", which Falconer had mentally dubbed "Carmichael Towers" (which would also do as a physical description of the man himself, because, boy, did he tower) could only be reached by a back alley-way to the rear of the house. Falconer had attempted it once, after a downpour, and would not be repeating the experience, as he had practically ruined a very nice pair of hand-made Italian shoes.

Sounding his horn in a blaring flourish, he waited in the road outside the house until his — he could hardly bear to think the word — partner appeared; which he did within a few seconds, showing his usual flair for fashion and style. Today he was in tartan trews and a Deep Purple tee-shirt, a disreputable black leather jacket, considerably scuffed, completing the outfit.

Falconer looked at his Acting "Watson" and sighed deeply. Sherlock Holmes never had to lead a docile bull around with him. There was no whiff of the bovine about Dr John H., who had always had his dependable service revolver with him when in a tight situation. As, in fact did Holmes himself. Falconer absent-mindedly frisked himself as he experienced these thoughts, then leant across to open the passenger door.

"Sorry about this, sir," Carmichael said, before Falconer had had the chance to speak, "only, it's me mam's wash day, and you know what it's like in our

115

place — apart from my uniform, I'm sometimes surprised I don't have to go out in my sisters' clothes."

"God forbid!" his superior replied, slipping the car into gear, and trying to ban from his mind any visual image produced by Carmichael's last remark. It was just too beastly to imagine — Carmichael in drag!

"How old are you, Carmichael?" he asked as they headed towards the village of Stoney Cross.

"Twenty-seven, sir," his passenger replied, keeping his eyes on the road in front; in fact imagining he was driving this much-coveted car, and having to fight the urge to make "broom-broom" noises as his superior changed gear and accelerated.

"Good grief! I thought you were much younger than that."

"I joined straight from school, sir, and I'm working for my sergeant's exams at the moment."

Falconer nearly veered off the road towards a ditch as he heard this. If Carmichael won his stripes, he might be moved permanently into plain clothes; they might become long-term partners. He shuddered at the thought, and decided he'd have to ask for a divorce. He and Carmichael would suffer from irreconcilable differences, and no judge could fail to grant him his decree.

Changing the subject, the inspector asked Carmichael what he thought about the decline in British farming over the past few decades, as they were now driving through the countryside, and the silence in the vehicle was giving him the willies. He found his passenger surprisingly knowledgeable on the subject, finishing with the statement that he used to work on a farm in the school holidays.

"But, how?" Falconer questioned, not knowing how to phrase his question tactfully.

"What? How did I manage to work on a farm when I was brought up in a council house?"

"Well, yes, I suppose so."

"I 'ad a bike!" explained the acting sergeant, a smug smile on his face at having outwitted a superior officer.

III

DI Harry Falconer parked his car in the car park of The Inn on the Green, realising that this was the best place to start off. Landlords knew everybody and everything that went on in a village, and the original 999 call had been made by a Mr Peregrine McKnight, of this very address.

When they entered the bar they found it full, an unusual occurrence for this time of day, even on a Friday. Summer had been heard yelling herself back to The Inn after her visit to her father's house, and word spread in a village, better than soft butter on a slice of freshly-baked bread. All those who had been involved in the Festival were present, some with alcoholic drinks, others with soft drinks or coffee, but all gathered together, united in confusion and dismay at what had transpired, and anger at what had been publicly broadcast that afternoon.

That none of them regretted Marcus's death was a given; that they all regretted that it had happened in

117

their village was also true. The words "some maniac passing through" and "some other poor git he'd vilified in the past" had been spoken by a few, but there was a general feeling of vulnerability in the air. The residents of Stoney Cross were the latest victims to be knocked down in Marcus's verbal coconut shy, and they herded together now, like nervous animals, seeking comfort and safety in numbers, unaware of this as an instinctive action of self-preservation.

Initially invited into the back room to follow on from Peregrine's 999 call, Falconer paused a moment, asking everyone present that, should they wish to leave, would they also be good enough to leave a note of their name, address, and a telephone number where they could be contacted, with Acting DS Carmichael, whose hulking form and intimidating attempt at plain clothes were cowing some of the more nervous souls present. So saying, he went behind the bar and disappeared through a door between two lines of optics, to find himself in a small, but exquisitely decorated and furnished sitting room.

Looking around the room in quickly suppressed surprise, his first question was about how Peregrine had received news of the death. After the explanation that their paying guest was the victim's daughter and had visited her father, only to find him in no state to receive her, Falconer wanted to know where the young lady in question was now.

"She's upstairs in her room having a lie down," Peregrine explained, but when Falconer asked for directions, he was given a look of discouragement. "I wouldn't, if I were you, not just now, anyway."

"Why ever not?" Falconer was puzzled at this reluctance to let him at the finder of the body — his prime witness, as she now was.

"Because the young lady was in a bit of an hysterical state, and Tarquin — my business partner — has got these tablets for his insomnia . . ."

"You didn't give her one?" Falconer was aghast, then blushed at the way he had worded his question. "A tablet, that is," he added, somehow making things worse.

"Two, actually." Peregrine had the grace to blush at his foolishness. "Sorry, old chap, didn't think. Just wanted to stop her yelling and calm her down a bit. I know she's not used to them, so you'll probably get no sense out of her till the morning."

Falconer felt like throwing a tantrum. "Good God, man! Don't you see what you've done? You've nobbled my witness, like a bloody race horse in the Grand National. You've obstructed my investigation, held up my questioning, and have caused a gross waste of police time — and that last one's a criminal offence, buddy." He was incandescent at the stupidity of the man.

"Sorry, old son," was Peregrine's only answer, and, though he didn't like it, Falconer knew he was going to have to damned well lump it.

"Right, let's get it on with Joe Public out in the saloon," he declared, with a weak attempt at humour, and exited the little room to return to Carmichael.

The arrival of The Police (very much with initial capitalised) had had a remarkable effect on the fullness of the bar, and when Falconer re-joined his partner, Carmichael had a considerable list of contact details, but was in the company of only one other, who turned out to be Tarquin of the Tablets, as Falconer now thought of him. He could add no more details to Summer's return to The Inn but, as one half of the eyes and ears of the village, was willing to go through Carmichael's list with them, and give them some details of to whom they referred: little thumb-nail sketches to get them going. Well, it was better than nothing, and the three of them sat down at a table, to be joined, almost instantly, by Peregrine, now recovered from his "bollocking", and eager to add his two-penn'orth.

Both halves of The Inn's management loved the opportunity to dish a little dirt, when offered it on a plate, as it were. In their opinion, gossip made the world go round. Money was just a rather pleasant "extra", and they eagerly provided details of their customers, each interrupting the other in his enjoyment of the activity. About the Festival, they were very forthcoming, and when the two detectives left the premises, it was with a full load of "stuff" with which to challenge their interviewees, should that be necessary.

First, however, they needed to visit The Old Barn to view the body. A local PC had been entrusted with the role of "guard dog", scene-of-crime officers had arrived shortly afterwards (not having had to change into less expensive clothes first!), and Falconer and Carmichael were eager to join them and learn what they could from the body and its locus.

CHAPTER
ELEVEN

Friday, 11th September — later that afternoon — and early evening

I

As they entered the drive of The Old Barn, the now-sorry sight of Marcus's beloved phallic symbol, his TVR, greeted them. All four tyres had been slashed, and it sat well down on its haunches. In addition, a sharp object had been used to give some un-commissioned art work to the long sleek bonnet. In unsteady scratches were the words "world's biggest prick"; so the victim had not been Mr Popular, then. Noting these desecrations, Falconer and his "mock-Scot" sidekick made their preparations to enter the actual scene of the crime.

Having changed into the required white forensic suits, overshoes (there had been none large enough for Carmichael's size fifteen feet, and he had had to settle for one pair on the toes of his shoes, and one pair on the heels, both held together by tape, to stop him contaminating the locus), and all the other gubbins involved these days with entering a crime scene, they

122

ducked under the blue-and-white tape fluttering its "keep out" warning, eager to see exactly what had happened. Falconer and Carmichael entered the house, to be immediately confronted with what looked like a bizarre scene from a modern "blood, guts and gore" crime story.

They had entered by the French windows, finding themselves in a good-sized room with a desk, an office chair, a sofa, and a sea of boxes, some unopened, others in the process of being unpacked. A few of the smaller ones that had been by the desk were on their side, their contents spewing out onto the floor. The desk lamp was still lit, and Marcus Willoughby was slumped in its light, his head on the desk, the deep depression on his skull seemingly spot-lit, above a red sheet of blood. Round his neck was a ladies' silk stocking, tied very tightly from behind, then formed into a bow, as if he were gift-wrapped, ready to be presented to his Maker.

The computer monitor was a few inches from his white-stubbled scalp, the keyboard moved to the right-hand side of him. If he had been using it when he was killed, he must have typed as if he were playing the very top notes of a piano, with his body slewed to the right at an extremely uncomfortable angle.

His face was purple, his tongue protruding, and when, with permission from the SOCOs, Falconer lifted the head he could see that the side which had rested on the desk was an even darker colour — from post-mortem lividity, he had no doubt. Someone had evidently wanted to do a thorough job on this chap, and had staged it as a show-piece. He shuddered as he looked once more at the head wound and the stocking.

Casting his eyes down to one of the overturned boxes by the desk, he noticed a reflection of light from a metal surface, and immediately identified some common DIY tools. He had no idea whether one of these had been used to strike the death blow, or whether the stocking was applied first, and a blunt instrument had been used when the murder turned out to be a little more difficult than had been expected. It might even be that the blunt instrument had been brought to the crime scene by the murderer. At the moment, however, there was evidence to support either theory. All he knew was that Marcus Willoughby was as dead as a door-nail, and he had another case of murder on his hands.

The computer would be examined by the police, should they think it had played any part in his demise, and, given the fact that his recorded programme had reached its destination, and even been broadcast, there was a high possibility that it would be leaving its current home at The Old Barn for a very thorough examination. Falconer had spoken briefly to the show's producer on the evidence of the broadcast passed on by Peregrine, before he had left the office, and had placed his laptop in the boot of his car before he had left to change his clothes.

After an initial examination of the scene, Falconer sought a word with the attending doctor, who had been about to leave when they arrived. This individual had stayed behind for a word with the SOCOs and, as

Falconer approached him, turned and called, "Hello, Inspector. We meet again!"

With surprise, Falconer recognised Dr Philip Christmas, with whom he'd had dealings on the Castle Farthing case. "Hail fellow, well met!" he replied. "I didn't expect to run across you quite so soon, and in such similar circumstances."

"Case of proximity, I assure you. I share my surgery between three villages: Castle Farthing, Monday and Friday; Stoney Cross, Tuesday and Thursday, in Corner Cottage just off the Market Darley Road; Steynham St Michael, Wednesday, and Saturday morning," he explained, long-windedly and unnecessarily. "I managed to wind up my appointments in Castle Farthing, and high-tailed it here as quickly as possible. I say, Inspector?"

"Yes?" replied Falconer.

"We really must stop meeting like this!"

For once, Falconer could think of no reply, but noticed the twinkle in the doctor's eyes, and grinned. They had shared an honest and open professional relationship in the aforementioned case, and the inspector felt reassured that things would remain the same for the duration of this one. Making his farewell, he returned to Carmichael with the beginnings of a feeling of familiarity — like an old team at a reunion — and hoped it would last. He stopped for a short while before leaving, to think.

He now knew that the initial opinion on cause of death was either strangulation, or trauma from a blunt instrument, that the time of death, nay, the day of death, for this was not a recent incident, was believed to be Sunday the sixth or perhaps Monday the seventh. It was too early to be any more precise without detailed evidence from the post mortem, but he ordered that this information be kept from public consumption for the time being, leaving him to be the judge as to whom, and when, he would let this detail out.

As the victim had lain there so long it would be interesting to see when anyone suspected of this crime would pitch their alibi — whether they'd go for the obvious assumption, that he had been killed on the night of Thursday the tenth, on the eve of the broadcast, or whether they'd have a cast-iron alibi in place for when the actual time of death was revealed. Of course, a clever murderer was capable of a bluff, or even a double-bluff, and a double alibi, but he hoped he would have the experience and instinct to see through anything of that sort.

Anyone who produced an alibi for Thursday was either innocent, or too damned clever. If they then produced a cast-iron alibi for the Sunday night as well, he was dealing with a smart bastard. Anyone who produced an alibi for just Sunday night was either the murderer, or simply telling the truth. At this point, he realised that he was merely confusing himself, and that these speculations were not helping him at all. What a tangled web there was, for him to unravel. He must remember not to get involved explaining these thoughts to Carmichael, or they would both be drawing their pensions before he had finished.

To Falconer's knowledge, from his visit to The Inn, Marcus had been in the pub on the evening of Sunday the sixth, until being ejected, about a quarter to eleven, so that shaved a bit off that estimate. Given that it would have taken only a short time to walk home — no, wait a minute, to stagger home, because he had been in his cups. That would have taken some time longer, and what if he hadn't gone straight home? And what if it was Monday? It was useless to speculate at this stage.

Stop being predictive, he told himself. First gather evidence, record it, correlate it, study it — then speculate like hell, if you can't see any pattern emerging. Gathering Carmichael on his way, they left the house, discarded their fancy dress costumes (in Carmichael's case, only the top layer), and Falconer went to the boot of his car to fetch his laptop.

Both settled in a fairly cramped manner in Falconer's car (for having Carmichael in his vehicle was a bit like giving a lift to a haystack), he played the podcast of that afternoon's programme, having downloaded it using the bonnet for a desk, there being no spare space inside the vehicle to do anything more active than breathe.

The voice of the dead man filled the air from beyond the Great Divide (in this case, the distance between Carsfold and Stoney Cross), Falconer diligently taking down names, as Marcus executed his character assassinations. His state of inebriation was soon discernible, and the two colleagues looked at each other for a fraction of a second. By the end of the broadcast — the ghastly end — they compared lists. The only name that didn't appear on both of them, with the obvious exceptions of husbands and partners, was that of Serena Lyddiard.

"Well, he certainly got choked off in no uncertain manner, didn't he, Carmichael?"

"He did indeed! And by the Grim Reaper himself. Best get started then, sir," suggested Carmichael, and, with a nod, Falconer switched on the ignition, preparatory to returning to the village and questioning those who had been maligned and insulted earlier that day, or perhaps more precisely, whenever this had been recorded. And that information would probably be on Marcus's computer.

II

There was no point, at the moment, in returning to The Inn on the Green, as Peregrine and Tarquin had not been mentioned in the programme, and their prime witness, Summer Leighton, had received a chemical cosh from her hosts, albeit innocently. Or perhaps not! "Trust no one" was one of Falconer's mottoes and may partly explain why he had never married, nor had a really serious relationship, by the age of forty.

He was astonished by their inability to find anyone at home. Those who had partners to answer the door for them explained away the absence of the other with tales of shopping or hairdresser's appointments. The married couples on the list were nowhere to be found, answering neither their doorbells nor their telephones. In fact, the only stroke of luck they had on this first foray into the society of Stoney Cross was a chance meeting with the vicar. He informed them that the Westinghalls and the Pargeters usually went into Carsfold late on Friday afternoons, the first family, to treat their brood to pizza, the second, for a visit to a burger bar.

Minty's and Sadie's absence he could not explain at all, but had he been a fly on the wall in each of their houses, he would have seen Minty lying on the floor beside a bed which was between her and the window. Sadie would have appeared as a dark, crouching shadow, lurking in the space under her stairs. Neither possessed the necessary sangfroid to speak to the police at the moment, as each of them had something to hide, and both shuddered at the sound of the doorbell and telephone, Minty having a little tremble, just for the hell of it.

They did, however, learn quite a lot from the Rev. Ravenscastle, who told them, with his anger at the memory still in his voice, of how he had found Willoughby in his church on the previous Sunday night. He also asked them not to bother Miss Horsfall-Ertz — "Everyone calls her Squirrel, because she's always at car-boot sales" — as she was very unwell at the moment, and he and his wife were trying to nurse her back to health with the help of some of her neighbours. He explained that it was not a case for a doctor, and related the tale of the Yorkshire terrier's death under the wheels of Marcus's car, and Squirrel's shock at seeing him again, actually in the village where she lived.

The reverend gentleman also added some very tasty snippets that might explain the number of deserted properties, where they had not been able to gain entrance. In the course of his duty of pastoral care, he had visited all those who had not been a roaring success at the Festival, thinking that they might need a few words of comfort in their embarrassment.

Sadie Palister had been, as expected, quite blasé about the whole thing, stating that she was sure the quality of her work would shine through anything that old poseur had to say about it. Minty Wingfield-Heyes had attempted the same hard attitude, then was struck with a fit of uncertainty, and unleashed a torrent of anxiety about what might happen if Marcus managed to poison the public against her work.

Rev. Ravenscastle had comforted her by reminding her that it was just a local radio station, but she had done her homework, phoning Radio Carsfold to be told that the programme was usually available as a podcast, and could be summoned up for consumption from anywhere in the world, for the next month. When the vicar left, she was still hugging her anguish to her, like a child with a dis-comfort blanket from which she could not be parted, not realising what the programme would contain, and in what bad taste it would be, to unleash this particular podcast on an unsuspecting world.

At each house at which Rev. Ravenscastle had called, he encountered pain and angry bluster, and dread at what Friday afternoon might bring. The two exceptions were at Starlings' Nest and The Haven. At the former, Delia and Ashley were almost light-hearted, poking fun at the whole episode, Delia commenting that she might have to claim late hay fever as the cause of her inaccurate blowing, and Ashley countering with a suggestion of hyperventilation, brought on by a terror of performing in front of a "national treasure", as he facetiously referred to Marcus.

At The Haven, however, he had encountered the other end of the spectrum. There, he had found Camilla Markland, alone, and steeped in grief. He could find no words to comfort her, nor explanation of her condition. Her face was flushed and puffy, her eyelids swollen so that her eyes were almost closed, and when he had mentioned Gregory's absence, she had convulsed into even more heart-wrenching sobs. After making her a cup of tea, the closest he got to an explanation was that they had had a little tiff, and Greg had gone for a drive to calm down. This was untrue, he sensed, but could elicit no further information without upsetting her more, and he had to leave her as he had found her, having provided no comfort, and learnt nothing about the cause of her wretched state.

At this point, Falconer and Carmichael were ready to move on with their, so far unsuccessful, house calls, and asked for directions to Blackbird Cottage and Serena Lyddiard, adding the hope that she, at least, might be in to receive them.

At the mention of Serena's name, the vicar smiled, and pointed them up Stoney Stile Lane. "She wasn't able to appear in our little show, though," he explained, in case they falsely believed otherwise. "She used to be a dancer, and everyone was so looking forward to her

131

performance. Unfortunately, however, she hurt her ankle in practice, and was unable to attend. We were all *so* disappointed. Well, I'd better let you get on with your job." And so saying, he left them, waving as he went.

III

Falconer and Carmichael made their way to Serena's front door, using the heavy brass "Hand of Fatima" knocker to announce their arrival. There was a disconcertingly long wait, and Falconer thought they had been stood up again, but soon, a shuffling noise was heard, approaching the other side of the door.

The door opened — and Falconer fell in love at first sight! There were no other words to describe what he felt. It was something totally beyond his comprehension; he had never experienced anything like *this*. His eyes widened, his pupils dilated, to take in the sight of her more fully, and he could feel his mouth hanging slightly agape. He was speechless for the second time that day, and stood there like a statue, drinking in her slender figure, her honey-coloured hair, her amber eyes, and the polite smile of enquiry on her face.

Carmichael, suddenly becoming aware that there was something amiss, made the introductions himself, casting swift sideways glances at the inspector to see if he could discern what had struck him dumb in such an inexplicable way. But learnt nothing, Serena not being his type; and too old, if it wasn't too impertinent a thought.

132

Falconer suddenly found his voice but, at first, it emerged in rather a husky manner, as he explained that they would like to have a word with her, and asked if they might come in, as having strange men standing on one's doorstep could be awkward, if witnessed by one's neighbours — and he wouldn't like to think that they had been the cause of any rumours or speculation . . . Whatever was he wittering on about? he thought, as he followed her into the house and into the sitting room. He was acting like a love-sick teenager, and had to check to see that his tongue wasn't hanging out, and he wasn't drooling.

"I am Detective Inspector Falconer," he began, in introduction, horrified to find that his voice had now risen to a high pitched pre-pubescent warble. Clearing his throat in embarrassment, he continued, "and this is Acting Detective Sergeant Carmichael." This came out in a strangled baritone, and he cleared his throat again, in an effort to pull himself together. "You, I presume, are Ms Serena Lyddiard." He had taken the precaution of using a hoarse whisper, and explained it away by claiming, unconvincingly, that he was suffering from a sore throat.

Carmichael was glancing at him again, in confusion. This was the first he'd heard of any throat condition — Falconer had been fine when they were talking to the vicar. As Serena nodded in acknowledgement of her identity, Carmichael stared outright at his superior, and said in a puzzled voice, "But, sir . . ."

"Not now, Carmichael!" Falconer admonished him breathily.

"But . . ."

"I said, *not now!*" Falconer did his best to shout, without engaging his vocal chords, but it just made him cough, at least supporting his claim that his throat was on the blink.

Waved towards the sofa, they sat down, while Serena lowered herself into an armchair and carefully placed her bandaged right ankle on a footstool, then looked invitingly towards them, awaiting an explanation of their visit.

Falconer was recovering a little and ventured, in what he hoped was his normal voice, "We're here in connection with the death of Marcus Willoughby; just making enquiries to establish when he was last seen, who might have spoken to him, that sort of thing, you know what I mean . . .?" There he went again, rambling, he really must get a grip.

Ignoring his discomfiture with a kindly discretion, she claimed her ignorance. "I'm afraid I never had the pleasure of meeting a man by the name of Marcus Willoughby."

"Not at all?" This was Carmichael, trying to cover up for Falconer's weird behaviour.

"I had my little accident," here she indicated her elevated leg, "just as he arrived in the village and, apart from my little trip to The Inn earlier in support of my friends, I've been more or less housebound ever since. I'm sorry I can't be of more help to you."

Falconer's body slumped with relief as he heard this, for the information filled him with an unaccustomed joy, and he had the sudden desire, fortunately

134

suppressed, to sing. Ms Lyddiard would probably treat it as a mild eccentricity, but Carmichael would know he was off his rocker, and that would do little for what tenuous authority he had over his giant tower of a colleague.

As they walked back to the car, Carmichael asked him what was wrong with him, and why he hadn't mentioned his indisposition before, as he had seemed perfectly all right earlier.

"Just a frog in my throat, Carmichael," Falconer explained unconvincingly, "Just a frog. Will you need picking up in the morning?" he asked, his vocal chords now returned to normal.

"No, sir. I'd be grateful if you'd drop me back home tonight, but I'm just going to pick up some clothes — me mam should have finished the washing by now, and I'll get first pick — then I'm off to Kerry's. She's making me my favourite meal, and the boys and us are going to watch a "Harry Potter" on DVD tonight. I'll be coming from her place in the morning, so I'll meet you here."

"You're a bit of a fast worker aren't you, Carmichael? You only met her a couple of months ago."

"You can't fight fate, sir, not when you meet your soulmate," Carmichael replied, showing an unexpected romantic side.

"No, I suppose you can't," replied Falconer, his mind back at Serena's house, imagining himself being suave and interesting, instead of acting like the bloody fool he had been feeling at the time. As an afterthought he added, "Do you like that Harry Potter stuff, then?"

"It doesn't matter either way to me. If I can see Kerry and the boys enjoying themselves, that's all I need."

For once, Harry Falconer envied his acting DS. It was a humbling experience.

Carmichael had met Kerry Long when he and Falconer were engaged on their previous murder investigation and, during and after the events in Castle Farthing, the two had grown increasingly close. She was grateful for a strong male influence in the household and had quickly become genuinely fond of him, as had her two young sons, referring to him as Uncle Davey now. Her vulnerability had brought out the best in Carmichael. He had initially wanted to protect her, and this had turned into love. He was a very happy acting detective sergeant. All the things about him that irritated Falconer, Kerry loved, treating his idiosyncrasies as endearing, and loving him all the more for them.

As Falconer suggested they meet back in the car park of The Inn on the Green on the morrow, he pondered what Carmichael's favourite meal could be. "Steak and chips" was his one and only guess. How he would have reacted had he known it to be spaghetti hoops on toast with grated cheese sprinkled on top (two platefuls!) we will never know.

What we can know, however, is that, for all his highfalutin tastes, Falconer loved nothing more, when he was feeling a bit off, than baked beans on toast, with lashings of brown sauce. This was something he used to eat in his teens, unaccompanied, at a mobile café in a

136

lay-by, fiercely keeping this guilty secret from his family and friends, for fear of their mockery and derision.

When he had dropped Carmichael off as required, he headed for home, a vision of orange and brown filling his mind, and a determination to eat his proposed delight well away from Mycroft, his seal-point Siamese, convinced that even a cat would see him in a different light, if he knew of this guilty indulgence.

CHAPTER
TWELVE

Saturday, 12th September — morning

I

Falconer's sleep had been disturbed in the past by night-mares of his time in the army, usually about the uncouth behaviour and the foul language of the squaddies. Tonight his disturbed slumber had an entirely novel cause. Every time he floated off into oblivion, he saw Serena's face and, as his dream-self gazed at it, he became aware that she was in some sort of danger. Danger from what, he never remembered, but on several occasions that night, he had awoken with a gasp, his whole body convulsing with fear, his pyjamas soaked with sweat.

Except for one occasion, when he was about five years old and his mother had been gravely ill, he had never felt such strong emotion for another human being, and he found it confusing and belittling. He could not believe he could feel so deeply and so much for someone after just one meeting, and even opened wide his mouth and gazed into the bathroom mirror at one point to check his throat, and work out whether he really was coming down with something.

The next morning found him tired and emotional (in the most sober way possible) and, after his shower, he opened his wardrobe door and realised he had not the remotest idea what to wear. Usually an outfit had already assembled itself while he slept, but his night had been so disturbed, that there was nothing waiting for him, sartorially, in the forefront of his mind.

He knew that, come what may, he would make some excuse to call at Blackbird Cottage sometime that day, and rashly decided to wear his favourite garments, in the hope that he would impress Serena with his good taste, and shore up his own self-confidence. A short while later he left for Stoney Cross, breakfast no part of this morning's schedule; his stomach was too full of butterflies for him to contemplate adding food to the mix.

It was fortunate for him that there was little traffic, for his inattentive driving could have been the cause of numerous accidents. As it was, he had a near-miss with a black cat as he drove down Stoney Cross's High Street towards his intended place of rendezvous. He winced as he swerved to avoid it, and cursed it for shaking him up like that. He was nervous enough without a black cat showing off just how "lucky" it really was.

The Boxster and the Skoda arrived virtually simultaneously, and the two detectives got out of their respective vehicles in a near-choreographed move, both stopping dead at the sight of the other, and staring in mirrored disbelief.

Carmichael stood there, immaculate in a dark grey suit, white shirt and lemon tie, his thatch of hair gelled into a respectable cap, the victim of a very recent shearing.

Falconer just stood there.

He was attired in black linen trousers (which had already creased on his drive over), a turquoise silk shirt (condition as yet unknown) which was frontally obscured by a canary yellow Shantung silk waistcoat, and decorated at the neck with a blood-red tie. The whole ensemble was finished off with a brown leather jacket which had cost him a small fortune in Italy, on a day when he had been feeling particularly frivolous and self-indulgent.

Carmichael's mouth gaped in amazement at this rainbow apparition that had, yesterday, been his elegantly attired boss, the undisputed king of the muted palette (with an occasional highlight of colour, just as a visual accent).

The acting DS was the first to recover his power of speech. "Nice threads, sir. What's the occasion?"

"Nothing, Carmichael. There *is* no occasion. I just felt like a little change. Is that all right with you?"

"Of course, sir. No offence intended, I'm sure. You look lovely and colourful."

"And what about you, Carmichael? What's with the Savile Row look?" Falconer asked, not really noticing how well his sergeant scrubbed up.

Had he done so, he might have seen the quite handsome young man that Kerry Long had fallen for. Carmichael had even allowed Kerry to persuade him to

140

let her tidy up his normally unruly hair, and today, he bore little resemblance to the ramshackle scarecrow who had first been partnered with Falconer only a couple of months ago. It wouldn't last, though — Carmichael's appearance had a mind of its own, and would soon revert to the norm.

"Marks and Sparks, sir — machine washable. I told you I'd get first pick if I collected my clobber last night."

"You should get first pick more often. You actually look the part today. Well done!" But Falconer spoke as if by remote control. His words were automatic, his mind still on how he could contrive a meeting with Serena.

They were to have no joy in The Inn, however, as Summer had risen early and gone out, not saying how long she would be gone. After her long, chemically-aided sleep, she was raring to go, and had had something very definite in mind as she had sailed through the door with her handbag swinging from her shoulder and a determined expression on her face.

"Did she say where she was going?" Falconer asked Peregrine, conscious that, for the second time that day, he was being eye-balled in a rather strange way.

"Sorry, Inspector, I couldn't say. She did call something. I think it was something to do with her brother, but Tarquin was squawking some Lady Gaga number, and I didn't catch it clearly. Yes, it definitely sounded like she was off to see her brother — something like that."

"Would you like to have a coffee before you go, Inspector?" Tarquin breezed into the bar from the back room, his movement checking for the merest fraction of a second as he espied Falconer's fancy dress. "Only, we've been gossip and news collecting — such busy little bees we are, aren't we? — and we thought you might be interested in what we've found out, didn't we, Perry?"

"Absolutely! Now, sit yourselves down, Tarquin and I will fetch a tray of coffee, and we can all have a lovely little chat." Both were a bit less butch than their "mine host" personae when in private, and it made Falconer and Carmichael squirm slightly in their seats in discomfort. Neither of them was particularly broad-minded, due in both cases to their upbringings, diverse as these had been.

When the coffee had been served, Peregrine opened the proceedings. "We've heard word on the grapevine that there's a deep dark secret in the bosom of our spiritual adviser," he began. "He — the Reverend Ravenscastle, that is — has been doing the rounds comforting everybody about anything that takes his fancy at the moment, but he's never let on about his and his wife's own personal tragedy."

"And it's directly concerned with Willoughby," Tarquin interrupted, eager to be a part of the story-telling. "His wife's sister's kid was killed crossing the road, by a drunken driver and . . ."

"And that drunken driver was Marcus Willoughby," Tarquin interrupted again.

142

"Ooh, who's telling this story, me or you?" Peregrine asked, bitchily.

"Both of us!" Tarquin declared, then added, "Now what do you think of that then, Inspector? Is that a motive for murder, or is that a motive for murder?"

"Don't be obscure, Tarka," Peregrine admonished him, and took over the question himself. "It's not a half-bad reason though, is it, Inspector? It's enough to drive anyone to kill, knowing that a little kiddie died just because someone didn't know when to stop pouring the stuff down his throat, isn't it?"

Mentally filing this juicy snippet away for further scrutiny, Falconer asked if there was anything further that they wished to tell him. He wanted to get out of this hole, away from the smell of stale booze, and the smell of long-ago smoked cigars which trickled through from the room at the back of the bar. He needed some fresh air, but was further delayed from satisfying this need by Tarquin, who whipped a newspaper from an adjacent table and thrust it at him. "Page twenty-two — the letters, hot off the press this morning."

Falconer shuffled the pages until he arrived at Letters to the Editor, and found a trio of contributions, from Mesdames Carstairs and Solomons, and a Mr Lionel Fitch:

"*Sir*, — presumptuous, as the editor — the editor in place — is in fact a Mrs Betty Sinclair, the actual editor being away on his annual holiday — *I wish to express my extreme dissatisfaction at the behaviour of Mr Marcus Willoughby, towards those hard-working (and unpaid) members of Stoney Cross who took part in the* recent *Arts Festival. I take exception to such rudeness and ignorance . . .*" Falconer read, out loud. "And two more almost identical offerings. I say, Willoughby didn't make friends easily, did he? First the vicar, now these three, and goodness knows how many more, after that programme of his. Quite impressive, in its way."

"It's no wonder somebody killed him, Inspector. It wanted doing!" Peregrine seemed to have an axe to grind, but, to mix metaphors, he was keeping his powder dry.

Getting his drift, but also keeping the lid firmly on his temper, Tarquin twitched back his newspaper and said that they mustn't keep them any longer, as they no doubt had a lot of "important investigating" to do.

Taking the hint, and eager to be gone from their present company, Falconer and Carmichael fairly fled outside, glad of the opportunity to get away, and get on with something else. Deciding to leave the vicar until last, they headed off for their second, and they hoped more successful, call of the day.

II

The first words that greeted them at The Old School made Falconer's stomach flip over, and his heart beat faster.

"I'm afraid I've done something very stupid . . ." Sadie Palister told them, a forlorn expression on her face. Had they found their killer so soon, so easily? The two men followed her into her kitchen, and the three of them settled down round the large wooden table, in silence.

144

"I'm so glad you've come. I didn't think I had such a persistent conscience," she began, "In fact, I didn't think I had a conscience at all. But, ever since the word got out that the old bastard was dead, I've been able to think of little else."

"Take your time, tell us slowly (a necessity, since Carmichael would be taking notes, and he didn't write very fast) about whatever it is you've done, and let us be the judges as to whether it's stupid or not." Falconer had experienced a frisson of excitement at the thought of an easy and swift solution to the case, and was almost holding his breath as Carmichael moved his chair slightly out of Sadie's sight-line, and discreetly removed his notebook and pen from his inner jacket pocket.

"It's just that I've had a run-in before with Willoughby, when he was the arts critic for the local paper. It was a couple of years ago now, but he was pretty negative — well, pretty vicious, if the truth be known — about my work."

Falconer did not try to hurry her, knowing that she needed to tell her story in full, if she was going to tell it at all. She continued, gesturing for them to follow her into her studio. "After he'd given me such a filthy review, I kind of got my secret revenge, and made this." At this point she pulled a covering from her statue "Art Critic" and just stood there, awaiting their reactions.

Carmichael slipped both notebook and pen into one hand, and used the other to cover his mouth. Falconer merely goggled for a second or two, cleared his throat, and asked, "Is this supposed to represent our victim?"

145

"Yes," Sadie admitted.

"Would you explain it to us, please?" Falconer could see what it represented physically, but needed some help to *interpret* what he was looking at.

Sadie made a breathy sound of inhalation, and began to enlighten them. "The base of the, uh, work, you notice, is upright and firm. This area represents what the, uh, subject, uh, sees himself to be: strong, hard, with obvious sexual overtones to represent his womanising, because he really was an old lecher. The, er, upper part, represents his weaknesses, which is, uh, obvious from the shape." Sadie was being uncharacteristically coy in her explanation, which Falconer could only attribute to her sense of guilt.

"You may have noticed," she continued, lowering her gaze to the appropriate level, that there are no, uh, testes . . ."

"But you've done the hair really great," Carmichael interrupted, not at all embarrassed now, and giving the sculpture a very close scrutiny.

"Thank you, but I digress. The lack of, uh, bollocks, if you'll excuse my language, gentlemen, is because the subject has — had — as it were — no balls. He found it easy to criticise and malign other people's efforts, either in print, or on the radio, as you will have heard recently, but he was too much of a coward to say anything face-to-face."

"Did he see this, Ms Palister?" asked Falconer, now biting his own lip in amusement at what Willoughby would have thought, coming face to face with something that made such a devastating comment on his character.

"He did! Last Sunday, when he was on the Artists Trail. He came here in the morning, and I could see him making surreptitious notes on his little recording device, no doubt just a few little snippets of spite — his usual modus operandi. Then he walked over here, I presume. I was in the kitchen at the time, so I didn't see his face, more's the pity, but I certainly heard him yelp. He sounded like a kicked puppy, and I came back to see — well, I *knew* he'd seen it. I just wanted to see his face. He'd caused me enough grief in the past, for me to want to see what it felt like for him, to be so harshly judged."

"Did his previous public criticism cause you any problems with your work?"

"It certainly did! Trade slackened off, and prospective clients who were about to agree to a commission suddenly backed off too, saying that they had changed their minds, or would need to think about it a bit longer. It took the best part of a year for business to pick up, and it was just ticking along nicely when *he* showed up. I couldn't have been more horrified if the Devil himself had turned up to review our little Festival."

"And what happened when you did see his face?" Falconer prompted, anxious now to get to the nub of the story — confession, whatever this was.

"He winged it! By the time I got in here, he was standing in front of a completely different exhibit, and when I asked him if he was OK, he said he'd stubbed his toe, the lying bastard. He'd seen it all right, and understood it. His face was all sort of mottled, as if it couldn't decide whether to go white with shock or purple with anger. He left shortly after that, but I knew I was in for it when he recorded his programme. I was in for a grand slating, make no mistake about that. And I got it, didn't I?"

"And?" Falconer frowned at her. "Is this statue the 'something stupid' that you've done, or is there something else we should know about?"

"Oh yes, there's something else," Sadie confirmed, her face flushing a little with embarrassment. "I'm afraid there is. I'd been in a bit of a stew since I knew he would be coming here, and after we'd all gone to the pub on Sunday night, I got a bit tiddly, went home, and got even more tiddly, and then, I'm ashamed to admit . . . I went up to his house, terrified he'd come out and find me, but just brave enough, because of the booze, to do it anyway. The mist gave me a kind of false courage as well. You did know it was misty, didn't you? If he'd come outside, he wouldn't have been able to recognise me with the poor visibility so, what with the booze *and* the mist, I had a fair chance of not getting caught." Catching sight of Falconer's face, she continued, "Yes, I'm just getting to the point. I'm afraid to say that I slashed all his car tyres, then slunk home like an animal, feeling just a tiny bit guilty."

Falconer sighed with disappointment. "You're absolutely definite that this was Sunday night?"

"Absolutely, because it was the day of the performances in the village hall, and I knew the next

148

week was going to be hell until Friday, when his programme was broadcast. The anticipation of his venom was driving me to distraction, so I thought I'd get him back first, before he got me, if you see what I mean."

"I understand. And I suppose you didn't try to see through any of the windows of his house?"

"No way, Inspector. There was a light on round the side of it, and I didn't want him to come roaring out with threats of the police and a charge of criminal damage."

"What time did this actually happen?"

Sadie took a moment or two to think about this. She had been bladdered. She had even fallen asleep for a while when she got back from The Inn, but she finally settled on about one-thirty a.m.

"Then you didn't realise that he might already have been dead when you arrived, his killer, perhaps, still on the premises?"

"You what?" Sadie stood with her mouth open, both hands rushing to cover it in her surprise. "When was he killed, then?"

"I'm afraid I'm not at liberty to disclose that information, for the time being," Falconer answered, pompously and somewhat irrelevantly, as he had already spilt the beans, "but you may take my word for it. Although I should be grateful if you would keep this to yourself, for you may have been in a very precarious position. If you had been recognised, the killer still in the house . . . Well, I should be very careful for the time being. Don't go out alone after dark, and keep your windows and doors locked. This could be a lot worse for you than just slashing a few tyres."

Falconer thought that the odds on his surmise being true were several thousand to one, but he had wanted to put the wind up her. She was a little too assertive for his liking and, truth be told, he found her just a bit intimidating.

Sadie had the grace to blush at this mention of her misdemeanour, and gave her word of honour most prettily. "When, exactly, did you last see Mr Willoughby alive?" Falconer queried, looking unconcerned as he waited for her answer.

"Not since he was asked to leave the pub, on Sunday night."

"Why was he asked to leave?"

"Oh, I'm sure someone else would get much more enjoyment out of telling you about that. Anyway, it was so distasteful that I really don't want to talk about it at the moment. If no one else says anything, feel free to come back, but I'm sure you'll get as many versions as you could possibly want from this gossip-ridden little community. I'm here for the fantastic accommodation I've got for my work, but my only real *friend* is Minty — Araminta Wingfield-Heyes, that is. She and I get on like a house on fire, and it's worth all the petty jealousies and back-biting just to have a laugh with her now and again."

Falconer and Carmichael took their leave, and used the time between visits to indulge in a little speculation. "Well, Carmichael, what do you think?"

"It sounded all right to me, sir, certainly sounded as if she was telling the truth."

"But she's an intelligent lady. What if she killed him — Sunday late to the early hours of Monday morning, the opinion is now — and then slashed the tyres to give her an excuse for being there? We'll have to see if Forensics turned up anything on her. It could just be a red herring."

Falconer was furiously trying to think. He'd need to get his mind tuned-in for his usual game of "Grass Thy Neighbour", but his concentration was constantly interrupted by visions of Serena's face, and the thought that he must find a good — or even a bad — excuse to see her today or he'd go mad.

"What was that, Carmichael?" He'd only been half listening. "Don't be so daft, man, of course there's no connection with fish in this case. Surely you know what a red herring is? You don't? Well, look it up then — I suggest you look at the titles of the books by Miss Dorothy L Sayers. You'll find a whole bunch of them there."

III

They were greeted at The Old Mill by a woman in floods of tears and in a state of extreme distress. After ascertaining that she was, indeed, Araminta Wingfield-Heyes and introducing themselves, her first words to them were, "I'm afraid I've done something very stupid!"

"We'd better come in, Miss Wingfield-Heyes, and then you can tell us all about it."

As they settled themselves in armchairs, Minty blew her nose trumpetingly, regained a little of her composure, and commenced to stare at Falconer with puzzlement. Rapidly checking that his flies were in order, he gave her a quizzical look, and asked if there was anything the matter.

"No, no," she denied, then added, "it's just that you remind me of something — I think it's your clothes. Oh yes, of course. I used to have a stuffed clown when I was little. Frightened the bejesus out of me, as I remember, but his outfit was the same colours as yours." Seeing his face, she rapidly added, "No offence, Inspector, but it's funny, the things you remember when you're a bit over-emotional."

Falconer frowned in astonishment. He'd chosen every garment very carefully — they were his favourite items of clothing. Whatever was the woman talking about?

"You said you'd done something very stupid. Would you mind telling us about it?" he asked kindly, deciding not to hold a grudge, as Serena's face floated, once more, before his mind's eye. He was becoming obsessed.

"It's about that horrible old man . . ." she started, then trailed off, not knowing what to say next.

"Go on. If you're going to tell anybody, it might as well be us," the inspector encouraged her.

"Well, if I start at the beginning, you'll maybe understand why I did what I did."

"A very good place to start, now off you go, Miss Wingfield-Heyes," Falconer prompted, glad to see that he had been right in assuming an unmarried state, and that she had not flown off the handle at being addressed as "Miss" rather than "Ms".

"OK! It all started over a year ago. I'd put some of my works in an exhibition — I'm an abstract artist, you know — and I was selling paintings, and doing, I thought, reasonably well. Then that old beast, Marcus Willoughby, gave me a stinking review in the local rag. I was so humiliated I didn't know what to do.

"There was no way I could see to fight back. It affected sales for months — and I did nowhere as well as I thought I would from the exhibition, because his review came out the day after it opened. I could have killed him with my own bare hands . . . Oh, no! I didn't mean that literally, it's just an expression. Of course I couldn't have actually killed him. I'm not that sort of person at all, and here I am rambling, making an utter fool of myself, as usual . . ." She was threatening to dissolve, once more, into tears

"Not at all, not at all!" Falconer had decided to be soothing, but it was Carmichael who did the most to restore her power of speech.

Getting up from an armchair, he walked over and sat down next to her on the sofa, gently putting an arm round her shoulders and patting the hand that lay between them on the leather. Although this would not have been a particularly sensible move if the witness was likely to bring an assault charge, Falconer did not think so in this case, and wondered why he hadn't thought of doing so himself.

Carmichael stayed on the sofa, but shuffled along to the end of it, so that his presence would not cramp her when she spoke, and she continued her story in a quiet, almost whispering voice.

"I hated him, from that time on. I couldn't believe it when Fiona — that's Fiona Pargeter. She lives at The Haven in Dragon Lane — when she asked him to come to review our efforts for his new radio show. He'd only done a few before that, but they were pretty poisonous — about people who moved to the country and converted old buildings," she used one hand to count, on the fingers of another, counting off the first.

"Let me see, he had a go at commuters who deserted the village and its facilities during the week." She marked off another finger, and continued, "He absolutely hated weekenders who brought all their provisions with them, and contributed nothing. He said they just used the villages as playgrounds for their second homes." Another finger was moved down. The fourth of her fingers went down as she added, "And he absolutely hated what he referred to as "incomers", as if it were a sin ever to move from one's place of birth.

"He had a real brass neck, considering that he's not from around here, *and* he bought The Old Barn, an obvious conversion, if ever I saw one. And the thought of *him* coming here and slating my work *again* was just ghastly. Imagine how much worse I felt when he actually *moved in*. I couldn't believe it! I knew I should have to move, sooner rather than later. Talk about rubbing my nose in it. And then I realised that I couldn't be the only one, by far, who felt like that about

154

him. He must have made loads of enemies, the way he rubbed everyone up the wrong way."

Here she paused to gather her thoughts, and Falconer sent her off, back on to the main track, for the information for which he had been waiting. "And what exactly was this 'very stupid thing' that you did?"

"Oh God, I still can't believe that I actually did it. Sorry, sorry . . . It was late Sunday night — well, to be more accurate, about half-past-one on Monday morning — and we'd all been in the pub, trying to drown our embarrassment. I was worked-up about losing customers again, and when I got home, I'm afraid I polished off a whole bottle of wine. Oh, not in one go, you understand, but slowly enough to keep me upright, and sufficient to make me bold and reckless.

"By the time I'd finished, I'd decided that someone should teach that revolting old man a lesson, and that that person should be me. I'd changed into my pyjamas when I'd first got in, and they happened to be black, so without another thought, I slipped on a pair of black shoes, put on a black headscarf — oh, it *does* sound ridiculous when I say it out loud! Then I crept along to The Old Barn and, with one of the knives I use for trimming my canvases, I scratched the words 'world's biggest prick' on the bonnet of his car, hoping, drunkenly, that he wouldn't mistakenly take it as a compliment. I must have been inspired by Sadie's piece of sculpture." Here she blushed, and hurried on, "It was quite difficult to see what I was doing; it was rather foggy. But I managed all right, in a sort of inebriated way."

"Did you notice whether the car's tyres were flat — had been slashed — at the time?" Falconer asked, giving rise to a look of confusion at this apparently irrelevant question.

"Did I notice what? No, of course I didn't. I wasn't in a fit state to notice anything. I was shit — sorry — terribly scared that he'd come out and catch me, because there was still a light showing at the side of the house, and I had visions of him hauling me off to the police station, drunk and guilty of criminal damage. The car could've been up on bricks, for all the notice I took. I was in a complete flap, but couldn't seem to stop myself."

Carmichael's pen ground to a halt shortly after she had finished speaking, and Falconer rose to take his leave, thanking her for being so honest with them. That was two, now, who had harboured a grudge against Willoughby, but their stories had a ring of truth about them. Unless, of course, they were in it together, and both the murder and the two acts of vandalism had taken place at the same time.

Falconer had the idea that they would be returning to The Old Mill before long, when its occupant was a little less stressed. It was just possible that, if she was not the murderer (or should that be "murderess"?), then she might have been scratching her little message when the real killer was actually on the premises, perhaps still inside the house, unable to escape because of her presence. Minty might have been in the same situation that he had just described to Sadie.

IV

Their next port of call was The Vicarage, to get the precise details of their previous family loss. If Willoughby had been responsible for the death of their young niece, then here was motive indeed. In fact, they seemed to be drowning in motives. Marcus must have been the most unpopular person in the village, if not the county. He ended his thought thus, remembering how Marcus's work had given him a much wider audience than most people had access to, to insult and infuriate.

Adella Ravenscastle opened the door to them, and led them into her husband's study, where he was still at work on his sermon for the next morning. "Time to take a break, Benedict. We have visitors. Inspector Falconer and Acting Detective Sergeant Carmichael," she announced, indicating their presence just behind her. "I'll show them into the sitting room and make some tea, and you can go through with them to see how we can be of help." Her words were confident enough, but there was the tiniest tremor in her voice, as if she had guessed what was coming, and wasn't looking forward to it one little bit.

Falconer didn't beat about the bush, and as soon as they had sat down opened his questioning with, "I understand that a young relative of yours was killed in a road accident, and that the driver of the car — the drunk driver of the car — was Marcus Willoughby. Is that correct?" He had gone in hard in the hope that, with little time to gather his thoughts together,

157

Rev. Ravenscastle would be less than composed in his answers. But he wasn't to get away with it that easily.

"As it was the daughter of my wife's sister, I really think we should wait until she re-joins us, don't you?" [*As that same late, great comedian, previously paraphrased, would have said, "There's no answer to that!"*] And so they sat, in an uncomfortable silence, Falconer seething that he had lost control of the situation before he had had the chance to exploit it. Carmichael, untroubled by the wait, doodled Mickey Mouse faces in his notebook and thought about all the wonderful plans that he had for his future. Falconer's mind also drifted away from his present ire, and he thought of Serena again, and realised he was getting just a bit distracted, and really needed to concentrate on the job in hand.

Adella Ravenscastle broke their reveries when she entered with the tea tray five minutes later, the kettle having taken an unusually long time to boil. Setting it down on a low table, she urged her husband to be "mother", and asked how they could assist the officers, a challenging glint in her eyes.

"I'd like you to tell us about the accident that led to the death of your niece, please, Mrs Ravenscastle. I know this must be an uncomfortable and upsetting subject to you, but the details may prove relevant to our current investigations, making it, therefore, a necessary evil."

"I don't see what relevance it can possibly have. It was a long time ago, and the driver went to prison for what he had done."

158

"That driver — that drunken driver — being Marcus Willoughby," Falconer stated baldly.

"That is correct but, in the eyes of the law, he has been punished; about the eyes of God, I make no comment, that being between his soul and his Maker," she answered stoically.

"That may be so, but I shall still need to know the details, and what you thought of his punishment — in the eyes of the law," Falconer parried.

"His punishment, here on earth, was paltry in the extreme, but I have faith that he won't get off so lightly when he stands in judgement before He who sits upon the throne." Thirty-fifteen to the vicar's wife — Falconer's serve. He was deprived of the opportunity, however, as Benedict Ravenscastle, in the role of umpire, butted in, and suggested that, as talking about it would be too distressing for his wife, maybe she could be excused, to let him tell the sorry tale. Boy, could this vicar change his mind! First, they shouldn't discuss it *without* her, now they couldn't discuss it *in front* of her. What was he playing at?

Falconer, having been aced, didn't feel it suitable to press his case too hard at this stage of the investigation and dropped his hard-ball attitude, but gave in with bad grace. Adella Ravenscastle got up and left the room, twitching the cover off a bird-cage near the door on her way out.

"It was November the fifth, 2001," the vicar began, only to be interrupted by a coarse voice from the other end of the room.

159

"Uckoff!" it declaimed. "Uckoff! Uckoff! Uckoff!" All eyes turned in the direction of this unexpected contribution to the proceedings, Carmichael's eyes sparkling as they alighted on a parrot.

"It's only Captain Bligh," the vicar explained. "I was left him by an old gentleman in my previous parish, and I hadn't the heart to have him put down. They live to a terrific age, you know."

"Uckoff!" rang out again from the cage, followed by what sounded like a very oily human chuckle.

"Don't take any notice of him. It'll only encourage him," Benedict advised, comprehension dawning on him as to his wife's last action before leaving them. She had done it on purpose, the naughty girl, though he couldn't blame her. The bird could stay uncovered for the rest of this interview as far as he was concerned. He knew the police had a job to do, but it didn't seem right for them to come here, after all this time, and rake it all up again. It would have been Maria's eighteenth birthday tomorrow, had she lived, and they had already made plans to spend the day with Adella's sister, Meredith, and take flowers to the grave to mark the occasion.

"To continue," he resumed, "we were all — Adella, myself, Meredith, her husband, and Maria — we were all going to the firework display in the town where my sister-in-law's family live. We'd almost got to the green, had just one more road to cross, when someone — obviously not from the display team — let off a rocket. A poor thing it was, but it was enough to get Maria excited. She thought the display had started without her, and that she was missing it, so she darted straight over the road towards the display area. Of course . . ."

"Uckoff! Uckoff!" That bird couldn't leave it alone. It was determined to undermine Falconer's authority, and destroy the sombre atmosphere.

"I expect he's jealous because your plumage is more colourful than his," the vicar said, with an absolutely straight face. "Shut up, Bligh! Can't you hear I'm talking?" he shouted, turning his head slightly to one side, for he could not, even in these circumstances, fail to see the funny side of the situation.

"Uckoff!" Captain Bligh replied, then he again added his almost human chuckle.

They're in collusion, Falconer thought. I don't know how they do it, but that bird knows exactly what it's supposed to do, and it's enjoying doing it. He longed for some superglue for its beak. That'd shut the damned thing up, no problem.

"Sorry about that. Now," he paused, "oh yes — but, unfortunately, she never got to the other side of the road." The recollection of this event sobered the vicar, and he continued, in a more subdued manner, "There was absolutely nothing that any of us could have done. She shot off so quickly. There was a screech of brakes, a thump, and our darling niece was dead. What more can I say?"

"Arse!" The parrot had found a new sound to play with, but Falconer had decided to ignore it completely, and not be side-tracked by its interruptions.

"Did you or your wife ever harbour feelings of revenge?" he asked, without much hope of a positive reply.

"We prayed for his soul, Inspector, and the gift of forgiveness, so that we could be at peace, but we're both still dreadfully upset by it, and, since that man came to the village, Adella's been having nightmares again. We're both good Christian people, but it's one thing to hate someone, and quite another to actually take a life."

"Can you tell me where you were on Sunday evening last?" It might be a bit of a give-away (again!), but he doubted the vicar would notice, so distracted was he by memories, and Falconer didn't think the reverend gentleman would talk about his interview with them to another soul.

"I went out for a while."

"And why was that?" Falconer had just noticed that Carmichael was no longer taking notes, and had deserted his duties to gaze enviously and with awe at the foul-mouthed parrot.

"Uckoff! Arse!" The inspector knew instinctively that the bird was playing up to an attentive audience, and summoned his (acting) partner back to his duties with a ferocious frown. "There was a bit of a disturbance at the church," Benedict answered him, undeterred. "Nothing of much note, just something that I had to sort out."

"Something we should know about? I think you'd better tell us anyway, and leave it for us to decide," Falconer advised, stressing the "us" and glaring afresh at Carmichael.

Looking somewhat uncomfortable at this turn of events, the vicar related his encounter with Marcus in the church, excusing the man's behaviour because he was "in his cups".

"Willoughby? Again?" the inspector cut in. "And how did this make you feel, considering how another of his little binges had previously affected your family?"

"It's not my place to be judgemental. Now, if that's everything, I do have a sermon to finish." He was giving them the elbow; the old heave-ho.

"As it will not concern the events surrounding your niece's death, I wonder if we could ask your wife a question before we go?"

"If what you say is truthful, I see no reason why not." As the Rev. Ravenscastle opened the door, the black-and-brown shape of a Dachshund scuttled into the room, bared its teeth, attempted to widdle on Falconer's favourite trousers, and, not succeeding, grabbed the material in its mouth and proceeded to growl as ferociously as such a small dog can.

"Hello, little doggie!" Carmichael cried with delight, reaching down to pet the animal's head, only to have his hand snapped at, and receive a diabolical glare back.

Little doggie, my arse, Falconer thought, longing to kick the little sod where it would have difficulty licking, given the elongated shape of its breed, but having to content himself with a slight shake of the leg and a sick smile.

"Just ignore him, Inspector. It's only our little Satan. He wouldn't hurt a fly, would you, my little hoochie-coochie?"

Cheeky old bugger, Falconer decided, envisaging a scene where he got the vicar in a dark corner and

163

scragged him, as Adella was summoned back to the hall, her grim expression dissolving into barely repressed amusement at the sight of his predicament.

"I wonder if you could tell me where you were on Sunday evening and during the early hours of Monday morning?" he asked, his face a mask of innocence, expecting to get confirmation of her husband's story.

"I went out for a little walk to clear my head," was her unexpected answer, and when asked to clarify this statement, she merely added, "I had something to do, and I wanted to do it there and then, while it was still uppermost in my mind."

She refused to give any explanation of her cryptic remarks and, short of arresting her, which was a ludicrous idea, they had to leave it at that. As they walked down the hall and out of the front door, the derisive sound of, "Uckoff! Arse! Arse!" floated after them; a final oily chuckle providing the full-stop to punctuate their uncomfortable stay in The Vicarage.

Closing the door firmly, Benedict turned to his wife and said, "Damned good idea of yours to take the cover off Captain Bligh's cage, but you are a very naughty girl, aren't you?"

"I know Benedict, but you wouldn't have me any other way, would you?"

"No, I wouldn't, and you spiked their guns good and proper. Good girl!"

Walking down the path and out on to the pavement, Falconer berated Carmichael for his unprofessional dereliction of duty, and roundly cursed "that bloody bird", as he referred to it.

164

"Sorry, sir, but I've never seen a real live parrot before only on the telly. I wanted to have a closer look. I reckon me and Kerry could do worse than have one of those for a pet."

"Heaven help you if you do. You'll never get a word in, with a feathery little sod like that. Why don't you do something normal and get a cat, or a dog? And what's all this about 'me and Kerry'?"

"Don't know about a cat, sir. They sort of give me the creeps — make me think of witches and that." He was totally unaware of the hostile glare his superior threw at him at this terrible slur on the domestic feline species, and continued, oblivious, "Dog wouldn't be too bad, if that sweet little doggie from the last place was anything to go by. And as for 'me and Kerry'," Carmichael tapped the side of his nose with his right index finger, and refused to say another word, as they walked towards Falconer's car, which they had picked up en route from The Old Mill to The Vicarage.

V

Retracing their route, they arrived at The Old Chapel just as Christobel and Jeremy Templeton had finished their lunch, and were immediately shown into a large living room, decorated and dressed in a very feminine fashion, no doubt the influence of the lady of the house.

They had no sooner sat down, having refused Jeremy's offer of coffee, when Christobel gave a little moan and, when they looked over at her, was found to

165

have her eyes filled with tears which were on the point of spilling down her cheeks.

Falconer eyed her with concern, asking her if they had called at a bad time. It was Jeremy who answered, however, pointing out that his wife had suffered a severely humiliating episode at the Festival performance, and had barely begun to get over that, when that "blasted radio programme" had plunged her back into a deep depression. At that point, Christobel rose from her seat and rushed from the room sobbing, and they could hear her hurried footsteps on the stairs as she fled to somewhere more private, to be alone with her misery.

"That bloody man!" exclaimed Jeremy. "I could've wrung his bloody neck for him!" He followed this outburst with a crestfallen look and, "I say, I'm most awfully sorry. I didn't mean that literally. It's just the way he treated poor little Chrissie's effort makes my blood boil."

"He didn't like it, I assume?" This was going to run and run, this theme, Falconer thought. Having listened to the podcast of the programme, he wondered in how many other households he would be told exactly the same thing. Although he and Carmichael had compared lists in the car, it had never crossed his mind to actually count the number of people who'd been cut to ribbons by Willoughby's tongue, but he guessed he'd know the answer to that one before the day was out.

"He hated it! Of course, I knew it wasn't really any good, but she's so insecure, I thought that her poetry would give her some self-confidence; some self-worth.

166

How stupid could I be? I could have cut out my own tongue when she said she was going to read a selection of her poems for this bloody Festival and, short of pushing her down the stairs and putting her in hospital, I couldn't see any way to stop her.

"I could hardly have told her the truth. She would have seen that as a betrayal by the person she trusted most in the world. I feel like an absolute heel. I should have done something — anything — to prevent her making a fool of herself in public. I can see another course of anti-depressants looming on the horizon, if Dr Christmas is obliging enough to prescribe them.

"I thought she'd coped with it when she said she was going to write a book and kill the bugger off in it, but she lost all confidence in her abilities again, when she realised the complexities of plotting such a long work, after just producing a little light verse, and we're back to square one now."

"I see your predicament," Falconer sympathised, trying not to interrupt the flow of the words too much.

"If it had just been a village affair — no bloody broadcasting outsider with improbably high expectations . . ."

"I don't think it was high expectations that made Mr Willoughby say what he did," Falconer interrupted, in an effort to offer support and comfort. "From what I've learnt of his character, I think it was just sheer spite, denigrating other people's efforts in areas where he couldn't hope to compete. It seemed that insult and contumely were his only two talents." This was a longer speech than Falconer had intended, but Christobel had looked so frail, and her sobs could still be heard, a muted background to their conversation.

"I'm sorry," Jeremy apologised again, "but she's a complete wreck, yesterday's programme almost sending her over the edge. Her nerve just broke. She actually threw the radio across the room and stamped on it, so distressed was she, and I had to put her to bed with a sleeping pill before she'd even heard what he had to say about her. She was so scared of hearing him criticise her, that she just descended into hysterics."

There seemed to be nothing here for them, in Falconer's opinion, and they said their goodbyes, the sobbing still emanating from upstairs as they left the property.

It was now well past noon, and they returned to The Inn on the Green for a bite to eat, and to check whether Summer Leighton had turned up yet. Food, they found; the discoverer of the body, they did not.

CHAPTER
THIRTEEN

Saturday, 12th September — afternoon

I

After their pie and chips (no Chicken Kiev, Falconer had decided, as he was determined to call on Serena later, and did not want to fell her with his garlic breath), they parked outside Blacksmith's Cottage in Church Lane, to have a word with the Marklands. Camilla had given a less than enthusiastically received harp recital at the Festival, and he wanted to gauge her reaction to Marcus's critique of it. Would she be wounded, as Christobel had been, offended, as some others were, or would she not give a tuppenny damn? Surely there was someone in this community who wasn't as thin-skinned as most of the others he had spoken to?

But, it was not to be. When they settled into yet another living room, Camilla's eyes were red and swollen, and Gregory's face displayed a thunderous expression, promising stormy times, either just ahead, or in the recent past.

Camilla, like Christobel before her, could not rouse herself to speech, and left all the talking to Gregory,

169

watching him with an anxious expression as he did so. "Camilla just had a bit of a problem with her instrument — nothing wrong with that. She's a very accomplished musician, and has given many recitals in the past — haven't you, *my dearest?*" There was scorn and resentment in this quest for confirmation, and Camilla merely nodded, before dropping her gaze towards her hands, which twisted and twined in her lap, as if giving expression to her barely suppressed desire to escape from the situation.

Waiting for no answer from his wife, Gregory continued, "Camilla's very obliging when her talents are being sought, aren't you, *my love?*"

The sub-text was unreadable, but Falconer had to give it a go. "Had either of you met Mr Willoughby before last week?"

"No." A barely audible negative issued from behind Camilla's concealing curtain of brittle, bleached hair.

"No!" Gregory's answer was almost a shout, and he clapped a hand to his mouth in an effort to stop himself saying more.

"Are you both absolutely sure of that?" Falconer was aware that he was being lied to, and in a very obvious and inexpert manner, but he wasn't going to push it today. He'd rather wait — let them stew in their own juice for a while, knowing that he knew they were hiding something.

"Yes." Their answers were simultaneous, and in as normal a tone as they could summon up. Falconer nodded at Carmichael, who put his notebook back into his inner jacket pocket and stood up.

"We won't take up any more of your valuable time today, but I may need to come back to ask you some

170

more questions." And that was that. They marched out of the house and back to the car without another word, or a backward glance.

Back in the car, Falconer spoke. "What do you think, Carmichael?" It would be good to have another opinion on what he thought of the situation.

"I still think I'd like a parrot, sir. A cat or dog's all right, but not so exotic . . ." He trailed off as he turned and saw Falconer's expression. "Sorry, sir! What do I think about what?"

"Oh, never mind! Where are we going next?"

II

Hugo and Felicity Westinghall ushered them into The Old Rectory, the former with a smile, the latter with a wince of pain, instantly suppressed. Their two children were sent out into the garden to play while Falconer conducted his questioning, lest little ears . . . etc.

Falconer knew damned well that in the secret world of children, there was more information than their parents would believe, and half of which they didn't know themselves, but if this couple hadn't learnt that yet he was not going to educate them. The little devils would be innocently hanging about, within listening distance, but looking totally uninterested, while they filed away any useful information to share with their friends and gloat over.

There was, however, little to learn here, except the inevitable distress caused by Willoughby with regard to Felicity's reading. The only surprise, which wasn't

171

really a surprise at all, as they had listened to the recorded programme, was Hugo's unexpected singling-out for praise. But this was batted away from the conversation, Hugo keeping his eye constantly on his wife, should she show any adverse reaction or jealousy.

She rallied, however, towards the end of the visit. The fact that Marcus was dead probably helped to reboot her self-delusion for, just before they were thinking of leaving, she chipped in with, "I'm sure the man was an intellectual moron, no appreciation of the arts and the finer things in life, I fear," and smiled a watery smile at the three of them.

Having spoken, she now seemed to find it hard to stop, and told them of the vicar's visit to Squirrel during the week, and of the parlous state in which he had found both her and her little dog. This, she followed up with a graphic description of Marcus's unexpected drenching at the refreshment tables on Sunday, (with Hugo butting in self-importantly to inform them of the incident with the knife), the reason for Squirrel's fury, and the poor woman's profound grief.

It had, initially seemed a pointless visit, but had produced, at the end, this cascade of information, mentioned by nobody else so far, and was grist to their mill.

III

Lydia Culverwell, at Journey's End, confirmed what Felicity had told them, but apart from a vicious diatribe on the state of the piano in the village hall, and the difficulties she had encountered trying to practise on "that ill-tuned device from hell", she had nothing more to offer, and they left her in peace, no new ideas to chew over.

"I wonder if that old lady was batty enough to have another go at Willoughby," Falconer wondered out loud, referring to the information they had gleaned from Felicity Westinghall.

"I understand people can get as fond of pets as they can of kids," Carmichael contributed, thinking of Kerry's two boys.

"They certainly can." Falconer was picturing his darling Mycroft, lying dead on the road, and tears came unexpectedly to his eyes. Damn it! he thought. This ridiculous over-sentimentality is all due to Serena and the way she makes me feel. I really need to get a grip. But at the thought of the object of his desire, he was transported back to the pink and fluffy world that surrounded her memory for him, and in which there were perambulators and pink-cheeked amber-eyed cherubs, with the same honey-coloured hair as their mother.

". . . to next, sir?"

"Pardon, Carmichael?" God, he'd got it bad, he decided, as he hauled his thoughts back to the here and now and the job in hand.

"I just asked where you wanted to go next, sir," Carmichael said, giving his superior what passed from him as a worried look, but would have looked more like

173

a grimace to anybody else. "Do you want to go straight to this Miss Horseyfill-Airs woman?"

"That's Horsfall-Ertz, Carmichael, and no, I don't. We'll call at The Haven and Starlings' Nest while we're up this way."

"And at Ms Lyddiard's?" Carmichael wanted to get the route straight in what he thought of as his mind.

"Definitely not!" Falconer declared, in a rather too vehement way. "We'll leave her till last," and was unaware that he was straightening his tie and running his hand over his hair as he spoke.

IV

Fiona Pargeter, as the original summoner of Marcus Willoughby, did have the conscience to display a little guilt at her part in setting up the tragedy, and she greeted them at the door with a crestfallen countenance, beckoning for them to follow her through to the conservatory, where Rollo was reading a newspaper.

"I had no idea what the consequences would be," she began in explanation, after the necessary introductions had been made. "I thought it would be so good to get a bit of publicity, and if we got a good review, it would be a good foundation on which to build — to, perhaps, make this an annual affair." Here she shuddered, and looked to Rollo for support. He acknowledged her mute appeal, and nodded for her to go on.

"I had no idea the man already had so many enemies in Stoney Cross, nor did I realise that he would make so many new ones when he arrived. I *do* feel, in part, responsible, but then, he was moving into The Old Barn anyway."

"Precisely!" exclaimed her husband. "If he'd had nothing to do with the Festival, it wouldn't have been long before somebody got to him. I keep telling Fi that this has less to do with her actions, and everything to do with the sort of man he was. He hardly had a fan club, did he?"

"Quite right, Mr Pargeter," Falconer agreed. "But then, I doubt if he planned on being murdered. Rather than apportioning blame, it would be more beneficial if we concentrated on who killed him. This may sound a little pompous, but I strongly disapprove of murder. No one has the right to take another person's life, and it's my job to track down those who cross the line to commit the gravest crime that exists in our society."

There he went again, running off at the mouth like a Sunday-school teacher. He definitely wasn't feeling himself. Maybe he really *was* coming down with something. All that he could think about, though, was that, after this, there were only two more visits to make, and he would see Serena again. First love is very painful — and he was suffering middle-aged agonies at its pangs.

Neither of the Marklands had been out much that week, except for work commitments. Socialising had definitely not been on their agenda, and they had little to add to what Carmichael already had in his notebook, (this being recorded in a weird shorthand of his own devising, and consisting of squiggles, weird hieroglyphs, and strange shapes — not too far away from what Mr Pitman had devised, then!)

There were, however, revelations to be gleaned at Starlings' Nest.

V

Delia Jephcott was so relieved that Ashley had taken her news so well, that she was in high spirits, and actually poked fun at her own incompetent performance the previous Sunday. "There I was, screeching and squawking away, feeling absolutely humiliated, but so puffed up with self-importance that I just couldn't stop, and had to carry on to the bitter end. How deluded I was. Time for a few singing lessons, I think, or a totally new hobby." She almost glowed as she made this declaration, smiling and bobbing her head coquettishly to one side in disbelief at her own self-delusion.

"Bloody good idea!" Ashley concurred, smiling, but growing more serious as he added, "Delia, darling, I think you should share your little secret with the inspector, now that you've let me in on it."

"If you say so," she agreed, and rearranged her features into a more serious expression. "I used to be married to Marcus Willoughby — there, I've said it!"

"What!!" Falconer was totally stunned by this unexpected revelation, and Carmichael stood staring at her, his eyes like saucers and his mouth slightly open (he was a bit adenoidal, however, so this was a fairly frequent occurrence).

"When? How? *Why?*" This last interrogative had been a slip of the tongue on Falconer's part, for she was quite an attractive woman, and years younger than

176

Willoughby. And Willoughby was by all accounts a revolting character to boot.

Answering the questions in the order that they had been asked, Delia offered up the information willingly, as if glad to get it off her chest at last. "About twenty or more years ago, I can't remember the exact date, but when I was a mere 'gel'. In a register office. And because I thought I loved him. We'd only known each other a month, and three months later I was gone, and had reverted back to my maiden name. I'd made a huge mistake, and have regretted it ever since. And he recognised me immediately, you know; he didn't even need to hear my name. I knew he'd put pressure on me if I wanted it kept quiet, and I had no intentions of being blackmailed by that slimy old pervert."

Her confession was greeted with absolute silence, and Ashley broke it, asking if they would like a cup of coffee. "Yes please, Mr Rushton," was all that Falconer could manage. A nod of the head was all that Carmichael offered, scribbling like the very devil in his notebook, lest he forget any of the details before he could commit them to paper.

But that was not all they were going to learn at this house-call. When they were sipping their Blue Mountain, Delia asked them if anyone had told them why Marcus was thrown out of The Inn on Sunday night. Hearing that no one had beaten her to it, she filled in the details for them with great pleasure.

"He was all 'hail fellow, well met, got to keep a stiff upper lip, don't let the buggers grind you down' when he got there, but he'd already had a few by then. When

177

it got to the point where he'd obviously had enough, Peregrine refused to serve him, which he had every right to do as a responsible landlord. And then he just went off on one, used some *filthy* homophobic language, and generally created such a hateful scene that it took five of them to get him through the door and on his way.

"I don't know whether Perry and Tarquin were offended, but I bloody well would have been. What business was it of his, how they lived their lives? They're both consenting adults and were free to choose whatever lifestyle they wanted. They've bothered no one here, and no one's bothered them."

Phew! Falconer thought. It was raining motives, and he was going to have to make a little list when he got back to the office. Name, motive, means, and opportunity. Four columns should do it.

"He could be bloody unpleasant when he was 'in his cups'," Delia added. "It's one of the very many reasons I left him."

VI

"I'm afraid I've done something very stupid!" Squirrel Horsfall-Ertz greeted them, her elderly features bunched into a grimace of remorse.

"Then you'd better tell us about it, hadn't you," Falconer asked, giving a mighty sigh. This admission had scored a hat-trick today, but it was becoming tedious in its inability to produce an honest-to-God confession about the murder. The first time, he'd been

178

really excited. The second time, a little less so. Now, it was becoming run of the mill — the recurring theme that would stamp Stoney Cross in his memory for a long time to come. "And about your little fallings out with Marcus Willoughby, with a knife, and then with a cup of tea. I'm afraid we already know about these incidents. I just need confirmation from you, if you'd be so kind."

"If he hadn't gorn and driven so fast, and murdered my poor little Bubble, that wouldn't 'ave happened." At Falconer's puzzled frown, she added by way of explanation, "Bubble was a little Yorkie. Him and Squeak were from the same litter, and they were inseparable."

At the sound of his name, the little dog scuttled into the room and, eyeing Falconer in his "Amazing Dreamcoat" outfit, headed straight for him, and started to worry at a trouser leg. "He's only being friendly," Squirrel explained, in the way that dog and cat owners always excuse the destructive behaviour of their beloved pets. "He just wants to play."

"Well I'm on duty, Miss Horsfall-Ertz, so if you wouldn't mind, perhaps, putting him out in the garden, I'd be very grateful." God only knew what state his trousers would be like when he got home. This was the second dog that had fancied them for a little game today.

Puzzled but compliant, Squirrel did as she was told, returned to the room and resumed her tale. "It happened last March. In Carsfold," she began, tears forming over her faded-denim eyes. "We'd been shopping, and were just going to the bus stop to come home for our tea —

I'd bought the boys a little pack of minced steak as a treat . . ."

She stopped, unable to hold back the tears any longer, and they spilt down her cheeks unchecked, her nose beginning to run in sympathy. Falconer handed her a clean handkerchief. He had a particular aversion to badly behaved noses, and he could throw the defiled hanky in the bin when he got home.

"When you're ready," he said quietly, hoping she would pull herself together. He'd had rather a lot of emotions to deal with today, not least his own disconcerting feelings, and he was eager to get away to their final destination.

Sniffing, she took up her tale where she had left off. "We were just crossing the road to the bus stop, when there was this enormous roar of an engine. I looked up, saw the car careering towards us, and stepped back, trying to pull on the leads to save the boys, they being a bit in front of me, like, because of the leads. Squeak was on the left, and I managed to get him out of the way, but Bubble, being just that tiny bit closer to the car, wasn't so lucky. Right under the wheels he went, such a tiny little thing — squashed flat! I never thought I'd see the day when I had to witness something that horrible."

At this point, she dissolved into sobs, and Carmichael went off in search of the kitchen to make a pot of tea. They would be there some time if they were to get the story to date, because that would mean calming the old lady down, and that wasn't going to happen in five minutes. His prediction proved to be

180

correct, and it was a quarter of an hour before Squirrel could resume her tale with any coherence.

"I knew his face as soon as I saw him again. You've got to report it to the police if you hit a dog, and I made sure someone from the crowd called them. Didn't want him to get away with it, see? And when he came towards me on the refreshments table, I couldn't help myself. Both times it was a reflex reaction. And I think I might've been a bit rude as well. This cloud of fury just came over me."

"So what, apart from threatening someone with a knife," — she was too upset to notice the sarcasm in his voice — "and throwing the contents of a teacup over the same person, have you done that's what you would call very stupid?"

Her eyes filled with tears again, and Falconer put one of his hands over her gnarled old knuckles in encouragement. They'd be here till midnight if she started howling again!

"I wished him dead, that's what I did. I wished it would happen, even prayed to God to strike him dead, and now he *is* dead, and it's *all my* fault," she wailed. Falconer's comforting hand had failed. What did Carmichael have that he lacked?

It was a further ten minutes before they could leave her on her own, and even then they called in at The Vicarage on their way to Stoney Stile Lane, to alert the vicar that one of his parishioners might be in need of his services again.

VII

As Falconer and Carmichael got out of the car and approached the house, the inspector was aware of a number of uncomfortable sensations. His stomach was turning cartwheels, his tie felt more like a noose, he had begun to sweat and prickle all over and he knew his face was as red as a sunset.

Unlike most people, he had not experienced these sensations at around the age of fourteen, and didn't recognise them for what they were — the symptoms of puppy love. At fourteen, he had been more interested in the CCF (Combined Cadet Force), intent on a career in the Forces even then. He'd had no time for socialising, or for girls. All his reading was on aspects of military life, and he single-mindedly kept things thus, until he had achieved his goal of joining the Army.

There hadn't been a lot of contact with the female form in his military years, and the contact that there had been had been dressed in regulation uniform, all signs of femininity and flirtatiousness trained out. He was similarly single-minded in his police work and, therefore, the impression that Serena had made on him was totally alien to his prior experience of life.

"Are you all right, sir?" Carmichael asked as they reached the front door.

"Absolutely fine," he replied, his tie feeling even tighter, his voice emerging as a strangled tenor. "Nothing to worry about at all: everything's just tickety-boo. I'm fine! Fine! Absolutely fine!" Realising he was rambling again and becoming a little too vehement, causing Carmichael to stare at him in a puzzled manner, he pulled himself together just as the door opened.

And there was the face that had caused this flood of emotion in him — that caused his heart to beat faster, his face to flush crimson, his mind to become a blank, and his loins to do more than just gird themselves.

Serena bade them enter and be seated, while she settled herself into the same chair as on the previous occasion they had called there, slightly changing the position of her footstool, before she elevated her left ankle to its well-stuffed, cushioned top. Carmichael suggested that he made them a drink, and, with the lady of the house's permission, set off to the kitchen.

Falconer cleared his throat, unable to think of a single thing to say, except for "I adore you", which hardly seemed appropriate this early in their acquaintance. Serena, noticing his discomfiture, threw him a lifeline by asking how the enquiry was going.

"Hrmph!" He cleared his throat again, then, "It's difficult to judge at this stage. We need to collate all the information before we can get any sort of picture of what actually happened." Once started, he couldn't stop. "There will, no doubt, be several possible scenarios to consider. Our job is to narrow it down to the one that probably occurred, then see if evidence is in existence to prove it. Only then will we be able to submit it to the Crown Prosecution Service, to see if we have sufficient proof to support a trial, and . . ."

He finally ground to a halt, not only running out of breath, but also of any idea of what he could possibly say next. He wanted to ask her out for a drink —

dammit, he wanted to marry her and father her children, but he could hardly blurt that out on a second visit. She'd think he was mad, and that's exactly how he felt — mad, out of control, and drunk with longing.

"Interesting mix of colours," she said, changing the subject in the face of his obvious embarrassment. "Do you always dress so flamboyantly?"

For the first time that day, he looked down at himself — *really* looked, felt his face flush again and, frantically searching for something to say in his defence, blurted out, "Terribly sorry, it is a bit bright, isn't it? Must've got dressed in the dark this morning, my mind completely away with the fairies." This explanation conjured up two pictures in his mind: one of Carmichael in his usual garb, and one of the landlords of The Inn on the Green, and he grimaced at these hellish twin visions.

Thankfully, Carmichael (the suave!) returned at that moment with a tray, causing a much-appreciated hiatus in the embarrassing proceedings and, after cups had been milked and sugared, tea poured and biscuits politely offered round, the questioning began.

Of course, it didn't last long, Serena pleading total ignorance because of her ankle, and her subsequent withdrawal from events surrounding the Festival, as she had done on their previous visit. Of Marcus, she claimed no knowledge at all. "I'm afraid that I have never met a Marcus Willoughby in my life, as I told you when we last met. Of course, I've had phone calls from friends in the village, keeping me up with the news and views, but I've been basically stuck here, kind people

184

doing my little bits of shopping for me, just waiting for the time when I can get back to normal."

"We completely understand, Ms Lyddiard, but should you think of anything that has been said, or that you've heard, please don't hesitate to ring me." Falconer drew out one of his cards and scribbled something on its reverse. "Here's my card, and I've put my home telephone number on the back, so that I can be available any time, day or night."

This brought Carmichael's head up with a start. He had been sitting staring into his cup, making strange adenoidal clicking noises at the back of his throat, but this had really caught his attention. He'd never known the boss to do anything like this before. The way he had dressed for today's interviews, his strange behaviour outside, and now this. A large smirk of comprehension spread across the acting sergeant's face, and he winked across at the inspector, his features contorting hideously in understanding, as he did so.

Falconer nervously cleared his throat once more, and rose to leave. The last thing he needed was Carmichael putting his blasted size fifteens into things. Before he knew it, the fool would be reciting "Falconer and Lyddiard under a tree, k-i-s-s-i-n-g." And he would die of embarrassment.

They took their leave as politely as possible, but once they were outside the garden gate, Falconer turned to Carmichael, who was grinning like an idiot, pointing at his superior, and sniggering under his breath. "One word from you, Acting DS Carmichael, and I'll bust you down so far, you'll be a uniformed foetus. You understand?"

"Yes, sir," Carmichael replied, but still looking like he had something to say.

"Don't even think about it, because it won't be pretty — ah-ah, no you don't — because it'll hurt you a lot more than it'll hurt me, and you've got your career to think of. Whatever would Kerry say, if she found out you'd done something very, very stupid?" he asked, turning the words they had heard so often that day, on his partner — now it was his turn to say them.

But, as Carmichael got back into his car to head for Castle Farthing, he was no longer smirking. There was a frown of confusion on his face. Something was wrong about today — he just couldn't think what, but it was nibbling away at the back of his mind. He simply couldn't get at it, at the moment, but something had been out of kilter. Something had been not quite right.

VIII

Back at home, Falconer paced up and down, unable to settle, and thoroughly rattled by his welter of emotions at their last interview. He found it impossible to concentrate on the case, so overwhelmed was he by the memory of Serena, the faint whiff of her flowery scent, and the loveliness of her face. It was no good, he couldn't go on in this distracted state. He had a serious job to do, but he also had to know if there was hope for him.

Trembling with fear lest he be rejected, he picked up the phone to speak to her. So shaken was he, that it took him three attempts to dial her number, and when she didn't pick up for four rings, he thought his head would burst with frustration. Having decided on this bold action, was he to be thwarted when he had finally dredged up the courage to speak openly to her?

The sound of her voice turned his knees to jelly, and he sat down abruptly, gathering his wits together to get it all off his chest. "Ms Lyddiard? It's DI Falconer here. This isn't an official call. I just needed to speak to you." He managed quite well in the end, given the circumstances, and although her final answer made his spirits soar, so high were his hopes, to other ears, it was quite ambiguous.

"I'm very flattered, of course. I don't, however, think it would be very professional for you to be seen in public, having a quiet drink with a possible suspect, while the investigation is in progress."

"But, would there be a problem for you afterwards?"

"Oh, afterwards is a completely different matter. Let's just wait, shall we, and see how things turn out?"

Falconer was in seventh heaven when he rang off, and he could feel his sense of judgement returning in the light of what he saw as an affirmative answer. She hadn't said "no". He took that as a "yes" and, as his head dropped with relief, he caught sight of his so carefully chosen attire and marched off to the bedroom to survey his length in the cheval glass.

"Oh, my God!" he exclaimed, the scales now fallen from his eyes. "I look like Carmichael after raiding my wardrobe. And I went out like this today and interviewed people. I must be a laughing stock in

Stoney Cross." The odd comments that had been made during their visits, making no sense at the time, suddenly did, rushing back to him in a wave of embarrassment.

"Damn, blast, bugger and bum!" he exclaimed loudly, and headed towards the shower to wash away his shame, determined to appear in more sober attire in the future, and happy in the knowledge that he would only have to wait until Monday to see Serena again. All those interviewed had been asked to drop into the station in Market Darley after the weekend to sign official statements, and Carmichael was probably, at this very minute, going through his notes to see what they had got from their home visits.

Getting back to business, he realised he had completed what he considered to be "round one" of the investigation. "Round two" would follow as surely as night followed day, and he had a feeling there would be a bit more "Grass Thy Neighbour" forthcoming within the next day or two.

After his shower, and feeling rather more like himself, apart from the "cat that's got the cream" grin slapped right across his face, he made two more phone calls, wrapped in a restrained burgundy-coloured terry-towelling robe, sober black slippers on his feet.

"Carmichael? What are you doing tomorrow? Quiet day with your young lady?"

"No, sir. She's spending the day with her godparents — Marian and Alan Warren-Browne from the post office in Castle Farthing. Remember them?"

"Lady with the headaches?"

188

"That's right, sir."

"Got any other plans?"

"Nope."

"Fancy a spot of unpaid overtime?"

"How could I resist, sir?" Was Carmichael developing a sense of humour?

"Back in the office first thing, then. I want all your notes typed up, and I want to take a good hard look at the large number of people who seem quite happy that our Mr Willoughby is permanently out of the way."

"Yes, sir. See you tomorrow morning, then."

His next call was to the editor of the *Carsfold Gazette*, the previous employer of Marcus Willoughby before he had started his ill-fated radio career. David Porter was always available on his mobile, in case a story was in the offing, Betty Sinclair, she of the edition with the disgruntled Letters to the Editor, had only been filling in for him while he was away on his late summer leave.

"Hello, David. Harry Falconer here. Look, I need a little favour, but it'll need a bit of trawling?"

"What's that, then? Got a scoop for me?"

"I read the "Letters to the Editor" page concerning a former employee of yours, and I just need to see any photographs you have of your ex-art critic, Marcus Willoughby — anything from his articles really. In fact, both photographs and articles would be rather good."

"You're pulling my leg; but then he always was more trouble than he was worth. Liked to be seen as all-knowing, and went out of his way to be controversial."

"No leg-pull involved, I assure you. I need to get more of a feel for the man, and not just the slewed spin of the people who've crossed his path."

"I'd heard he'd copped it. Have you got anything for me?"

"You know better than to ask that," Falconer admonished him, "and you also know that if you help me now, it'll be quid pro quo."

"Fair enough. You're the boss. I've got a green 'un just started working here, making the tea and running messages. I'll get him on to it; he's dead keen at the moment. Anything he finds, I'll get him to forward to you — I've got your e-mail address."

That was that, then. Tomorrow he'd use what they'd got today, see if a little tabulation would show up anything that wasn't obvious from the visits themselves.

CHAPTER
FOURTEEN

Sunday, 13th September — morning

I

Sunday morning found both Falconer and Carmichael back in the office, Carmichael getting his notes prepared for the file, Falconer sucking his pen thoughtfully (but not the inky end, as he had chided Carmichael about so doing), and about to put into writing the three things he needed to consider — means, motive and opportunity — for those to whom they had spoken the previous day. He began to write.

They had gone to The Inn on the Green first, so that gave him Peregrine McKnight and Tarquin Radcliffe to consider. There was no doubt that the old pub could probably have produced a club hammer (the probable blunt instrument), and with those two, even the lady's stocking wasn't out of the question, he thought waspishly. That was the means dealt with.

Motive was a bit trickier. He knew that they had been subject to a certain amount of homophobic abuse from Willoughby, but would this have provided them with enough reason to dispose of him? It was not out of

191

the question, if they had suffered similar harangues in the past from drunken customers; even from completely sober villagers who were less than tolerant of alternative lifestyles. Although there had been no mention of that sort of thing from anyone, that wasn't cast-iron proof that it hadn't happened. Perhaps Marcus had just been the last straw for one of them — or even both of them. One to use the hammer, the other to apply the stocking, just to make absolutely sure.

Opportunity was a given. Willoughby had, in all probability, been murdered after the pub had locked up for the night. It made no difference whether it was both, or just one of them. The one would surely cover for the other. Better leave them in the frame, then. Murder had been done for less — much less.

Next came Sadie Palister. She was reasonably tall for a woman, must be physically strong to carry out her work with stone, and there were, no doubt, any number of lethal implements lying around in her studio. She had also admitted to a strong antipathy towards the deceased, due to a previous review he had written about her work, and she didn't expect to be treated any more kindly this time, especially after she had left her "Art Critic" on display for him to find. She had also admitted slashing his car tyres in a drunken fury, on the very night he had been killed, *and* in the appropriate timeframe. Yes, she certainly had a motive, especially when you added artistic temperament, impulsiveness and booze into the mix.

As for opportunity, he had just noted the tyre-slashing incident, so that wrapped that one up nicely. Now, moving on . . .

Araminta Wingfield-Heyes had been the next to receive a visit. She had seemed very upset about what she had done to Willoughby's car, but that might just have been an act. He knew little about artists' tools, but he was willing to bet there was something heavy — either something to do with frames, or a stone pestle and mortar to hand, perhaps for grinding up paint (he was in complete ignorance here and clutching at straws). Even if it was not connected with art, there was probably something that could have been used. She had a car, so what was wrong with her having a jack or a tyre iron?

She had also received, in the past, a scathing review of her work which had affected her sales — so, ditto for Miss Wingfield-Heyes on motive and opportunity. How those two hadn't bumped into each other, he didn't know. He could only guess that their timing was slightly apart, and that the fog helped to conceal what the eye wasn't supposed to see.

He considered next the Reverend and Mrs Ravenscastle. There was a damned good motive there, but first things first. He liked to work, as he did everything else, methodically and in order. Means first, and his thoughts were drawn to the number of heavy crucifixes which could be found, not only in the church (for it had a small lady chapel as well), but in the vicarage itself. That would cover both of them.

Motive was obvious. Marcus had caused the death of Mrs Ravenscastle's niece — a ten-year-old, he recalled, happy and excited because she was going to watch the fireworks display, her whole life ahead of her, brimming with promise. What must her death have done to Mrs Ravenscastle's sister, and also to the Ravenscastles themselves? Here was a very meaty motive indeed, and he would probably have to bring them in for questioning — separately, of course. Who knew what dark thoughts of revenge lay festering in the hearts of even the most God-fearing and pious of people?

And there was that blasphemous outburst of Willoughby's in the church, after he had left the pub on Sunday night, to take into consideration. That must have left the reverend gentleman steaming mad, that Willoughby behaved in such a way in his church, after what the man had already done to his family.

That they had both been out of the house on the night in question had been freely admitted. And during the period of time in which the murder was probably committed. Because of the way the information was offered, they couldn't alibi each other like Peregrine and Tarquin, but he had no idea how strong they would be under interrogation. It must take a core of steel to live the life they lived, being so patient, considerate and forgiving. Falconer knew he couldn't have hacked it as a vicar. He'd have throttled someone within his first week in a parish.

His thoughts and his pen turned now to Christobel and Jeremy Templeton. Christobel was as skittish as a kitten, and seemed fragile and introverted. But looks could be deceptive, and the whole little world that her husband had encouraged her to build to boost her self-confidence had just come tumbling down around her ears. She didn't need to wait till Friday to know what Marcus would say about her verse.

That husband of hers was fiercely protective of her, as well. His anger at what had happened was plain to see. Did that anger turn to violence, to protect her? *Of course!* Why hadn't he thought of it before? Who could possibly have known that Willoughby had already recorded his programme — or as much of it as he had been permitted to — and that it had already been submitted to the radio station? In fact, *who* had done that? It must have been the murderer, and that person must have known *exactly* what he or she was doing. Another question for his merry band of suspects.

Here he was, in the middle of an investigation, and so distracted by his feelings for Serena, that he had not been thinking properly. Whoever killed Willoughby must have stopped the recording, done whatever was necessary (he had no idea what, and would have to find out — yet another phone call!) to forward it for broadcasting, and it would appear that it had been taken at face value, and not been listened to before it was broadcast. How macabre that had been! He'd speak to the controller of the radio station after he'd finished his notes.

He had one more criterion to fulfil before he finished with the Templetons, and he bent once more, to his task. Opportunity was an easy one. Either of them could have slipped out of the house, and if the other had noticed anything, would probably feel that it was justified homicide and would cover for the other partner.

There was definitely something going on between the Marklands, too, he had decided. The wife seemed very jumpy and tearful, her husband constantly on the point of losing his temper. It may not have anything to do with the case at all, but his instinct told him that it had, and he would have to dig a little deeper there to get to the bottom of it. As far as means, motive and opportunity went, however, he was stumped for the time being, and his pen started a new section, this time for the Westinghalls.

Hugo seemed a mild, good-humoured man who was happy with his lot, although writing romantic fiction did not seem, to Falconer, something that he, himself, could get much satisfaction out of. In some way, it didn't seem manly, and he was big on manly, due to his military background. Hugo was obviously making some sort of a living at it, however, if he managed to support a wife and two children. But his wife seemed to have made a bit of a fool of herself. Could the deflation of her ego, making her feel of so much less worth than her husband, have driven her to murder? No evidence as yet, m'lud, but she was definitely worth keeping in mind with the others he had selected as having potential for the role of "first murderer".

Ditto, he supposed for Lydia Culverwell. She lived on her own, so there was no one to say whether she had left the house that night with murder on her mind. He really had been very sloppy with his interviewing

196

technique, and upbraided himself for such dereliction of duty. Well, it wouldn't happen again, not with a date with Serena on the horizon; and the sooner he solved the case, the sooner that would happen.

At Starlings' Nest, he had been astounded to hear that Delia Jephcott had once been married to Willoughby, even if it had been years ago. She might have felt desperate to suppress the truth, maybe feeling that Mr Rushton, several years her junior, might up-sticks and leave her, after such a heinous suppression of her past. She had not seemed particularly bothered about it now, but she had evidently "fessed up" to Rushton, and he must just have taken it in his stride. But exactly when did she tell him? That would be a very interesting thing to know.

The gays — no, strike that — the guys at The Inn had said that their guest, Summer Leighton, had referred to Willoughby as her father. *What if the girl was the fruit of the marriage between him and Delia Jephcott?* Maybe Delia had told her partner only half the story. If the girl had been given up for adoption, it was obvious that she had traced her father. What if she was now on the hunt for her mother? Some women were a bit odd about children they had given up for adoption. Perhaps Ms Jephcott was one such woman, and would go to any lengths to conceal her parenthood. Here was food for thought indeed.

That just left him with Miss Horsfall-Ertz to consider. She may have got herself into a parlous state, but she was still broken-hearted at the death of her dog under the wheels of Willoughby's car. Was she capable, at nearly eighty, of taking a heavy implement, and bashing a man's head in with it? It was certainly not beyond the bounds of possibility, for she was no wisp of a woman, and, despite the arthritis, he realised that strong emotion can engender surprising physical strength in those who feel it.

That was about it then, for now. They had called on Serena last, but she had not been involved in the Festival at all, due to her injury, and she said she had never come across Marcus before — thank God she was free from suspicion, and he could live in hope that a drink might lead to a more meaningful relationship.

As he put down his pen, two things happened simultaneously. His computer indicated that he was in receipt of an e-mail, and the telephone on his desk gave just a single ring, indicating that Bob Bryant from the front desk wanted to speak to him.

It seemed always to be Bob Bryant on the desk, he thought, whatever time of day or night it was. There was some joking amongst the younger uniforms, that he had been there since the station was built — in fact, that it had been built around him — sometime about nineteen hundred, and that he was one of the Eternals, just passing time unobtrusively, until the end of the universe. But Falconer thought it more likely that he just didn't have much of a home life, and preferred to be at the station.

Lifting the handset, he learnt that Peregrine McKnight was on an outside line, wanting to talk to him urgently and, as he waited for the call to be put through, he idly wondered what he could possibly have to tell him, calling for Carmichael to come and check his computer. It had not yet been twenty-four hours since he had spoken to David Porter but, if his luck was in, he might have come up with something already.

II

Peregrine's voice sounded in his ear, shrill with concern. "That Summer Leighton never came back last night — you know, that girl you wanted to speak to? We'd given her a latch key when she checked in, so we just went to bed when we'd done the rest of the locking up, but when I went to her room this morning with a cup of tea, the bed hadn't been slept in, and I don't know what to do about it."

"Rule number one," advised Falconer, "is don't panic! She's an adult, and I think you said that she was going to see her brother."

"I'm not completely sure what she said, now. She sort of called it over her shoulder. It might have been her brother, but now that I think about it, I really don't know any more."

"Have you got a home address or a telephone number for her — preferably mobile?"

"I don't know. I don't think so. No. After everything that happened after she arrived on Friday, it simply slipped my mind. And she was off and out before I got a chance to talk to her, yesterday."

"How very careless of you!" Falconer was definitely not impressed with this sloppiness on the part of a landlord, especially with respect to fire regulations.

"Let's see, she's actually been gone, and completely out of contact now for, what? — a little over twenty-four hours? Look, let me know, in the meantime, if she shows up. If not, I'll call over and take a look in her room, see if she's left us any clues. But I don't want either of you going in there. Do I make myself clear?"

"As crystal, dear heart," on which dubious endearment Falconer put the phone down.

As he replaced the handset, Carmichael was standing beside him, like a pointer dog indicating the kill. His left forefinger was extended towards the screen of Falconer's computer, an expression of smug intelligence on his face.

The inspector had been right, and the e-mail *was* from David Porter. The particularly juicy item that was on his screen at the moment was a photograph of Marcus Willoughby, his arm around the shoulder of Camilla Markland, her slightly vacant (and clearly drunken) face smiling up at him adoringly. What a find!

"She lied to us, sir! She said she'd never met him before!" Carmichael was righteously indignant.

"How perceptive of you, Sergeant, and do you realise what this means?"

"That it could be the cause of all that bad atmosphere in their house, yesterday."

"You *are* getting good, it certainly could. But was this their first meeting, or was it a sort of reunion?"

"Don't understand, sir." Carmichael was certainly having to run through his repertoire of expressions this morning, and the face of the moment was "puzzled", or

200

"hideously gurning" depending on how well you knew him.

"I've just had a call from Mr McKnight at The Inn on the Green, and I might be putting two and two together and getting five but . . . Let me explain. This girl, Summer Leighton turns up in Stoney Cross and ends up finding our charmer, Willoughby, dead. That was Friday afternoon.

"On Saturday morning she leaves the pub, seemingly calling out that she was going to see her brother. Mr McKnight has just informed me that she never returned to The Inn last night. Yesterday, we find out that Ms Jephcott was married to Marcus — "twenty years or more" ago. I had already surmised that, if this Summer Leighton had traced her father, maybe it was her mother rather than her brother that she was going off to see. And I was about ready to put Ms Jephcott as a possibility in that role." It was all a bit muddly, as he listened to himself, but he knew what he meant, and so did Carmichael, he hoped.

"Now, you show me this picture, and I wonder if perhaps Madam Markland knew him from the past. First, Miss Leighton's father is murdered, then *she* disappears. I think we can also put la Markland in the frame, tentatively, as possibly being her mother. So, what have we got here?"

"A problem?" Carmichael was definitely not getting it.

"One of two stories. Think, man! Was Willoughby murdered out of pure hatred, for what he did professionally? Or was he murdered because he could reveal a past that someone wanted to suppress?"

"Dunno, sir. I give up."

"It's not a riddle, Carmichael. I want your opinion on which scent we ought to follow."

"Still dunno, sir."

"All right, at ease! Print me a couple of copies of this picture. We're going to have to go back to Stoney Cross to have a look at Miss Leighton's room at The Inn. We might as well take a copy of this picture with us, and just call in on the Marklands and that Jephcott woman again. They won't be expecting us, especially on a Sunday. There are two possible mothers in that village, and they ought not to be overlooked. And we ought to have another word with those other two women — Palister and Wingfield-Heyes, while we're there. Either of them, or even both of them, could have done anything, when they were all hyped up and on the lash."

And, God dammit, he'd have to speak to the radio station before he went any further. He needed to know how much expertise was needed to end and send the recording of Marcus's programme. Could it be done by someone who'd never done it before, or would it need expert knowledge? He had no idea, and picked the phone up to remedy this omission in his education.

And, good grief! Falconer realised that he and his acting sergeant were going out in public together, and surveyed Carmichael's attire accordingly. He knew it was supposed to have been his acting sergeant's day off, and he had agreed to come into the office and work overtime for no remuneration, but now they had to go out, Falconer looked at the young man's clothes in a completely different light. Anyone who hadn't already met them might think he was supervising Carmichael on the rare treat of a day out. Was, in fact, his carer. What that would do to his street cred, he dreaded to think.

III

The answer he had received from the radio station had got him no further forward than he was before. Someone who knew what they were doing with this particular software would have had no trouble at all. On the other hand, someone who had never used it before could have followed the step-by-step instructions, and have achieved the same end. He'd have to have been particularly cold-blooded, however, to have worked at that computer while Marcus lay dying or dead in the office chair beside him.

At this added frustration, Falconer arrived at The Inn on the Green in a fairly foul temper, not helped by Carmichael burbling happily from the passenger seat about how great life was now that he had someone to share it with.

Both Peregrine and Tarquin were ready for him, and Tarquin showed them Summer's car, still parked behind the pub in the rear car park, then Peregrine led them upstairs to the room she had booked, but only slept one night in. There wasn't much to be seen of her occupancy after such a short time, and it did not take them long to go through the few things in her holdall, and the toiletries left in the shower room, (for all the rooms were "en-suite").

Falconer was not going to be beaten that easily though, and he lifted the pillow from the bed to check beneath it, then stripped the duvet from it, to check under that. Next, he lifted the mattress and — bingo! There he found a black leather-covered diary, a pink Filofax, and an envelope.

The black diary was Marcus's, and the little minx must have pocketed it when she found his body. She was cool enough to do that, before she ran back to the village, screaming blue murder. The pink affair was Summer's own, personal diary. At a quick flick through, both of these recorded the coming together of father and daughter, and gave the name of her mother — Jennifer Linden, known as Jenny.

Which didn't offer much help — who the hell was Jenny Linden? How much easier it would have been, Falconer thought, if the mother had had the forename Delia, or Camilla. The contents of the envelope did nothing to enlighten him, either. This was a photo-copy of a birth certificate for someone called Polly Linden, not Summer Leighton, and the mother was listed as Jennifer Linden, the father as Norman Clegg. Who, in the name of blue blazes, were these two people? And, how did they fit into the case? — if indeed they did. Perhaps all this business about finding long-lost parents was just a mare's nest. On the other hand, Summer was definitely (possibly) missing, maybe abducted (or even dead), and must be treated as such, after a lapse of twenty-four hours since she had last been seen. Falconer was getting confused, with two other names entered on the race-card.

The other piece of paper helped slightly. It was a copy of an adoption certificate, for Polly Linden, a six-week-old baby, whom the adoptive parents had renamed Summer, their surname being Leighton. At least that tied up!

Feeling completely arsed-about by events, Falconer took out his mobile phone and prepared himself to speak to Detective Superintendent Chivers — on a Sunday! He wouldn't be best pleased, but the inspector needed his permission for staff to conduct a search of the surrounding area, and to make house-to-house calls. This couldn't be handled by just Carmichael and himself, and he wouldn't get any thanks if he didn't call this one in now, either.

CHAPTER
FIFTEEN

Sunday, 13th September — afternoon

I

Falconer had been right. Superintendent "Jelly" Chivers had *not* been pleased to be called away from his last barbecue of the season, and he made his feelings unequivocally known. He was a man who had come up through the ranks. No fast track for him. And he didn't mince his words.

"Why did this all have to bloody well blow up on a *Sunday*? You'd think a hard-working superintendent could be guaranteed one bloody day of peace a week. Stupid little bitch has probably got herself a bit of scrummy, and is at this very moment curled up in his bed, oblivious to all the bleeding trouble she's causing other people. Young people of today — (sigh!) — they don't give a bloody toss who they inconvenience, as long as they get their end away. Never tell anyone where they are, because they're too bleeding busy having fun. Too many rights, and not enough responsibilities, that's what they've got, these days . . ."

At this point, Falconer felt he had to interrupt. "She could hardly tell her father, sir, as he'd just been murdered. And part of the problem is that we don't know who her mother is, so we don't know whether Ms Leighton informed her or not."

"Damned careless of you!" Superintendent Chivers retorted unfairly, then gave his permission for uniformed officers from both Market Darley and Carsfold to be drafted in to start the search. "You're not going to be very popular though, disturbing some of them on their rest-day. Still, that's your problem, not mine. And get on to the local paper and radio stations as well, see if they can put out an appeal for the girl to get in touch, or for anyone who has seen her in the last twenty-four hours, etc., etc., etc. You know the form, Inspector. Now get on with it, so I can get back to my guests, and act like the genial host that I'm supposed to be."

Before Falconer could get another word in, the line went dead. He had been hung up on, which improved his mood not one jot. At least he had David Porter's number in his mobile now, just in case, and he could probably rely on him doing him the favour of getting in touch with any radio stations in the area. If he was after a scoop, he'd have to work for it. He'd know much better than Falconer what radio stations covered this area, and it would save him a bit of time. He could always confirm with them later on, if need be.

Falconer had a half-formed — or was it half-baked? — plan in his head, and it was in a much less gloomy state of mind that he listened to Carmichael's latest report from Happy-Ever-After-Land, while they took a look through the windows of Summer's car, waiting for reinforcements to arrive.

This took less time than he had anticipated, and within forty-five minutes (and two cups of coffee apiece) he had a dozen uniforms awaiting his instructions. Peregrine had also put out the word, and there were about a dozen men from the village at his disposal as well.

"Right," he started, thinking of the topography of Stoney Cross, "I want you in four groups of six; three police officers, the other three, civilians. I want the first group to go northwest, working its way across the sports pitch and into the copse beyond. Group two, same configuration, I want to head north-east, across Stoney Stile Lane." At each instruction he pointed in the direction given, lest any confusion arise.

"The third group, I want to go to the south-east, through the agricultural land; and the last group, south-west, starting at the standing stones. If you find anything, I want to be informed *immediately*. If not, I want you all back here at five o'clock to report. Uniforms, I shall want to brief you then, on the house-to-house calls. There are special instructions for this" — he smiled cryptically — "so I don't want any of you sloping off and doing your own thing. Have you got that?"

There was a ragged chorus of "yes" and "yes, sir", and he stood and watched as they sorted themselves out into groups, and decided which group should go in which direction, eventually moving off, an air of excitement about them, at this unexpected little adventure. Falconer didn't think they'd feel half so excited if they *did* find anything, but that wasn't his problem at the moment.

"Fancy a spot of lunch, Carmichael?" he asked. "I should think that'd be admissible on expenses." A final "yes, sir" reached his ears, and the two detectives left the car park and made their way back into the pub, which was, at that very moment, about to finish taking orders for roast beef and Yorkshire pud.

Carmichael was an incredible eater, Falconer thought, as they wrapped themselves round a delicious roast. He seemed to put his grub away with remarkable speed and efficiency. The most miraculous thing of all, though, was the way he seemed to be able to eat and talk at the same time, without choking himself, or even, it would appear, drawing breath.

"Can't believe it's happened to me," he finished, through a mouthful of roast potato, and looked to Falconer, for his opinion.

"What's happened to you? Sorry, I was concentrating on my plate." This was patently untrue, as he had been thinking of how he would bag the house-to-house call to Blackbird Cottage for his very own, but Carmichael wasn't to know that.

"Kerry wants me to move in with her."

"That's great news, Carmichael! I assume you've accepted."

"Sort of."

"What do you mean, 'sort of'? You've either accepted or you haven't, and if you haven't, you must be mad."

"I don't hold with all this living in sin, sir," Carmichael explained, a slightly pained expression on his face. "Me mam brought me up to know right from wrong — part of the reason I joined the Force — so I said I'd love to live with her, but only as her husband."

"You mean, you proposed to her?" Falconer was astounded that his frequently tongue-tied colleague should have either the old-fashioned morals, or the gumption, to make a proposal of marriage.

"I certainly did, sir. And she said 'yes'. We haven't set a date yet, but I shouldn't think it'd be too far in the future. Neither of us wants any fuss, and Kerry has been married before, as you already know, sir."

For a moment, Falconer was speechless, then he held out his hand to shake Carmichael's, and said, whole-heartedly, "Congratulations! I hope you'll both be very happy together — well, all four of you, I suppose I mean," he added, remembering Kerry Long's two young sons.

II

Finishing their meal, Falconer decided that they would call at The Vicarage first. There were a few things he wanted to try out there — see if he could budge their stories; perhaps surprise one of them into changing their story. He was glad that they had taken his car, as he hadn't relished another ride in Carmichael's Skoda dustbin, and Carmichael had been insistent that he didn't mind not taking his car as well. As he would be going over to Castle Farthing for the evening, he said it was no problem, so long as he could be dropped back at the station's car park to pick up his own. It would give him the chance to change into something a little less like work clothes [*more details later!*] for his evening with his prospective new family.

Work clothes?! Falconer thought, and could hardly believe his ears, but he held his tongue, not really sure whether Carmichael was "extracting the Michael", or was in deadly earnest.

On arriving at their destination, the inspector also insisted that they be shown into a room other than the one that contained the poisonous presence of Captain Bligh, and that the Dachshund, Satan, be banished to the kitchen. He didn't want a repeat of the shambles that had been their last visit there.

He had made a point of dressing more soberly today, so that his appearance would not be a source of fun. Carmichael, however, was another matter. His attire had been OK for the office, especially, as has been mentioned before, that this was one of his rare days off, but now they were back on the job, as it were, Falconer once more eyed him up and down critically.

Carmichael had, as so often in the past, gone his own way sartorially. He certainly had a style all his own, and Falconer suspected that it had less to do with his excuse of "first up, best dressed", and more to do with his own personal taste. He would have to pluck up the courage to ask him sometime, but shelved it for the moment, not feeling up to what the answer might be.

Carmichael's shirt was a day-glo orange, with scars of purple tie-dying here and there; his trousers, although well-fitting, were a shade of grass-green corduroy. His tie, in contrast to the sort of hippie life the rest of his attire suggested, was a little number from the mid-seventies, wide at the base, and depicting an oriental girl against a brown background.

Quietly humming the tune to "Aquarius" from *Hair* under his breath, Falconer thanked his lucky stars that they weren't on surveillance. If that situation ever arose, he really would have to give his acting sergeant a talking to, man-to-man. If only he would wear the suit, or a similar one, to the one he had worn yesterday, there would be no problem. As it was, Carmichael was like a mobile firework, drawing catcalls and wolf-whistles wherever they went, and was particularly amusing to very young children, who would point, and shriek with delight at the unexpected appearance of a clown in their otherwise predictable lives.

They sat, now, on a sadly sunken sofa in the vicar's study, Mr Chalk and Mr Cheese, awaiting their prey, on the busiest day of the reverend gentleman's working week.

When Reverend Ravenscastle did arrive, his mood was mixed. He was sorely vexed at being disturbed on the Sabbath, but also full of concern for the missing girl, and his first comment to them, after greetings had been exchanged, was that he had prayed for her safe return.

Falconer, who, at the moment, wasn't sure whether he was investigating a hate-murder, an abduction, a double murder, or some sort of combination of these events, was in no mood for ecclesiastical niceties, and

212

threw himself into questioning the man about what he had been doing, abroad on the night of Marcus's murder, with no alibi. He had become aware that somebody was leading him by the nose, but had no notion of whom that person may be, or in what way he was being led, at the moment, and it was affecting his temper.

"I've been through Army training, Reverend Ravenscastle, and I've been to war. I've seen apparently mild-mannered men turned into shouting, screaming killing machines. I've seen the glint of the savage in their eyes and in their behaviour. I know that civilisation is only a thin veneer, and I believe the same of religion. I also think it's more than possible that, after all the memories of the death of your niece that Willoughby's presence in this village brought back to you, the ill-will he had manifested in general, and the desecration and blasphemy that occurred in your church, you simply cracked. You threw aside the veneers, and reverted to the savage that dwells in all men's souls.

"I believe it was you who went to Marcus Willoughby's house on Sunday night, and took your revenge on him for all the sins he had visited on your little world." By the end of this, Falconer's voice was raised to a shout, and Adella Ravenscastle looked round the door to see if everything was all right.

Without looking in her direction, keeping his gaze fixed firmly on her husband, he spat, "Get out of here! And don't come back until I tell you to!" Causing her head to disappear, with a little yelp of surprise. Her husband opened his mouth to remonstrate, but Falconer silenced him with a word, holding his hand out in a gesture that meant, unmistakeably, "stop!"

"Murder!" He glared deep into the vicar's eyes, daring him to speak. "Thou shalt not kill," he quoted. We are investigating the taking of a human life here, the most heinous crime that can be committed. This is *your* territory, so I'm sure you understand that I *need* to find out who was responsible. Now, it's not my place to judge, but if that person was either you or your wife, I am duty bound to bring you to justice, and I will do everything within my power to uncover the truth — even shouting. Understand?"

"I do understand, Inspector. I was an Army chaplain, myself, at one time, and I have counselled broken men — men who were manipulated into doing or being what you have described, and I have seen their guilt and remorse, and the way that it haunts some of them, both sleeping and waking."

"Ah. I see. Sorry, Vicar! You obviously understand my situation. Is there any chance you were seen on Sunday night, while you were out?" Falconer had been put in his place after his outburst, and now spoke more contritely.

"Very little, I'm sorry to say. Stoney Cross generally goes to bed early, and it was very misty. Even if someone had chanced to look out of their window, I would just have been a dark, obscure shape to them. I can, however, assure you, with all the strength of my Christian faith, that I didn't go to The Old Barn, and that the only hand I laid on Marcus Willoughby was the pat on the shoulder I gave him, as I sent him on his way home from the church."

This bald statement had the ring of truth about it, but Falconer could not afford to ease up too much in his questioning. "I'd like to speak to your wife now. In the kitchen and alone, if you don't mind. Perhaps you would care to move your dog to another location for a few minutes?"

"No problem. I'll take him outside to see if he has any 'business' to conduct. Let me know when you've finished — and don't be too hard on Adella. It would have been our niece's eighteenth birthday today, and she's taking it hard. We're planning to visit Maria's grave with some flowers, later today, with Meredith and her husband, and it's going to be a very emotional occasion for all of us."

The inspector was checked by this information. He had intended to go in as hard with Adella as he had with her husband, initially, but he had the feeling that, with what he had just been told, it would be better to play on the wounds of emotion from which today's date had picked the scab. It might work in his favour — sometimes people were less able to keep up their guard under the influence of strong emotions.

He found "Mrs Vicar", as Carmichael had taken to referring to her, sitting on a plain oak chair by the kitchen table, her head bent, her shoulders shaking, and a tea-cloth pressed to her face as she wept. This was definitely a case of "softly, softly, catchee monkey". If he pressed her too hard, given the circumstances, there was the likelihood of a complaint being lodged, and then where would he be? Up Shit Creek without a paddle, that's where he'd be, and no mistake.

"I'm sorry about just now, Mrs Ravenscastle. I'm afraid I was rude to you, and there's no excuse for being rude to a member of the public."

She had not heard him come in, so sunk in her thoughts was she, and she jumped as she turned round in her chair to face him."

"I accept your apology, Inspector, and I'm sure that Benedict explained why I'm so upset, today, of all days."

"He did, and we quite understand." Carmichael had shambled into the room, and now loomed over Mrs Ravenscastle in a concerned way. Unexpectedly, he crouched down beside her and put an arm around her shoulders, speaking very quietly to her, so that Falconer was unable to catch his words. She just nodded and sniffed, listening with silent attention.

In a couple of minutes, Carmichael unfolded his length into an upright position, and went to stand beside the inspector again. Mrs Ravenscastle, the Lord be praised, was wiping her eyes and visibly pulling herself together. "That's a good young man you've got there, with a sensible head on his shoulders. He'll go far, mark my words," she announced, rising and putting on the kettle.

"Don't worry about tea for us, Mrs R." This was Carmichael again. "Make a pot when we've gone, then sit down with your husband, and you can share your memories and comfort each other."

216

Falconer was dumbfounded. Had the fairies come and changed his usual Carmichael for another one overnight? If they had, both Carmichaels had the same dress sense! — the same air of being a fashion victim, and simply not caring.

Mrs R, as the acting sergeant had just referred to her, sat down again, and told them calmly and frankly, that she could produce no witnesses to her walk on Sunday night, but that it had had a purpose — although not a murderous one. It was a secret at the moment, but if they would care to call round tomorrow, she would provide proof of her story, and also someone who would corroborate it.

As they strolled back towards the car, both in thoughtful mood, Falconer's mobile began to jingle, and he fished it out of his jacket pocket with the far-fetched hope that it might be Serena. It wasn't. Sadie Palister's forthright voice rang in his ear with what he considered unnecessary volume. "I've remembered something from Sunday night, but I don't know if it'll be of any use to you."

"We'll be straight round."

III

Sadie met them at the door, ushering them hurriedly into her studio and bidding them sit. "What is it that you've remembered?" asked Falconer, speaking in a rush in his eagerness to learn something new.

"I don't know if it'll be of any help at all, but I remembered I'd seen a car, or what I presumed was a car, and heard it too, when I was on my way back from The Old Barn." She had the grace to blush as she remembered why she had been abroad so late at night.

"Where did you see it? And what time was this?"

"I can't give you an exact time, Inspector, because I was too drunk even to focus on my watch, should I have had the urge to do so, so I stick by my approximation of about one-thirty in the morning, which is exactly what I told you the last time we spoke. But, where was I when I saw the car? That's it! I was just steadying myself to stagger down School Lane, when I heard the noise of an engine. Looking in that direction was just a reflex, but I got the impression of a vehicle moving very slowly towards me down the High Street, from the other end of the shops; from Dragon Lane way."

"And did you recognise either the car or the driver, Ms Palister?" Falconer's hope was slim but, without hope, what was the point of life? Serena's features swam before his mind's eye once more, and he had to quickly gather his attention, lest he miss her answer.

She was regarding him with a slightly sneering expression, her long black hair falling forward across her face. "Inspector, not only was I blind drunk, but it was also dark and foggy. Visibility was practically nil, and what's more, the car didn't have any lights on. Crawling along, it was, even slower than I was, and I was practically on my hands and knees by that time. I didn't even remember what I'd done that night till the next afternoon, and even then I wondered if it had all

218

been a very vivid dream — of course, I eventually realised it wasn't but, for a while, I was hopeful."

"And you're absolutely sure there's no way you could have a shot at saying whose car it was?"

"If I said I could, I'd be lying. I said that what I had remembered probably wasn't worth much, so I hope you didn't get your hopes up too high." There was that word again — hope. His had been dashed on this occasion; he "hoped" he would be luckier in other respects, later.

"Thank you, anyway, Ms Palister. I'll certainly add that to my case notes, in case something else comes up that might corroborate what you've told us." And with that, they left The Old School, Carmichael putting away his notebook in his Tango-coloured shirt pocket, Falconer muttering under his breath at his bad luck in the prevailing weather conditions on the night of the murder.

"Let's go grill these mothers," he decided, then qualified his statement, should there be any misunderstanding. "Alleged mothers-of-the-abducted, I mean," he amended, and turned his car towards Starlings' Nest, Delia Jephcott in his sights for his next shot.

IV

To Falconer's complete and utter surprise, Delia laughed in his face when he suggested that she and Marcus might have been the parents of the missing girl. Her laughter poured out in ringing peals, prolonged and musical, tears running down her face by the time she had regained control of herself. There was no sign of righteous indignation at all.

Ignoring this with as much dignity as he could muster, he continued undeterred. "Have you ever been known by the name Jennifer Linden? Have you changed your name by Deed Poll at any point in your life?"

Again, she seemed about to dissolve into amusement, but steadied herself by holding on to the back of the sofa. "I have absolutely no idea what you're talking about, or where you got these ridiculous ideas from, but I can assure you that the only name changes I have had have been when I was married to that twit Marcus, and when I reverted back to my maiden name, three months afterwards. And no, I don't know anyone who *is*, or who *was* called Jennifer Linden," she stated, forestalling his next question. "And if you must press the point, inconvenient as it will undoubtedly be, I shall voluntarily get a statement from my doctor, declaring that I have never borne a child. Would that suffice?"

It would, and Falconer felt a bit of a fool as he headed back to the car. Aware of a mutter from Carmichael, he asked him to repeat what he'd said, as he hadn't heard him. "I said, it was lucky that she didn't try to show you, that's all, sir," Carmichael intoned expressionlessly, but a little louder. Really! Falconer didn't know where to look. He'd die of embarrassment at the thought, if he had to speak to the woman again. He would have no idea where to focus his eyes. Was this another example of humour from his acting sergeant?

V

Their visit to Blacksmith's Cottage took a little longer than the previous one. Camilla and Gregory Markland still seemed ill at ease in each other's company, a palpable tension staining the atmosphere of the house. Camilla looked as if she had been crying again that day, and Gregory still had a look of brooding fury on his face which affected his body language and made him appear to be in an aggressive mood. Neither of them took a seat, when they had ushered in the two policemen.

Falconer decided that the best way to get results was to go in, cards straight down on the table, to see if he could get a result. "Mrs Markland, I need to ask you something, and I need you to tell me the truth."

The colour faded from Camilla's face, like the action of an ammonia solution on a piece of pink velvet, and her mouth puckered in self-defence. Gregory's stare hardened, until his eyes seemed to be made of steel, boring into the inspector's skull. Taking the photocopied photograph he had obtained from the Gazette, he handed it to her in silence. "I understood, from what you told me the last time I was here, that you and Marcus Willoughby had never met before. In the light of what I have just passed to you, would you care to revise that statement?"

Camilla began to shake, and, with a trembling hand, passed the photocopy to her husband. "I can explain . . ."

"I think you'd better. This is a murder enquiry, not a game of Cluedo, in case it had escaped your notice.

Somebody is dead, and I intend to find out who was responsible, no matter how many cages I have to rattle in search of that person."

"Oh God, I'm so sorry, Greg. I'm going to have to tell him," she moaned, staring at the carpet, not daring to meet her husband's eye.

"Do what you have to, but I don't have to be here to listen to it!" he spat, and stalked from the room. The front door could be heard slamming behind him, as he left the house in a mood that had moved swiftly from bad to infuriated.

"Go on, Mrs Markland. What have you got to say?"

"I met him after a concert last year — well, you know that; you've got the article and picture on that copy." She was still staring at the carpet, but, in her husband's absence, slowly raised her gaze until she was staring at a spot just above Falconer's head, still avoiding locking gazes with anyone, but regaining her composure a little.

"I, really stupidly, had far too much to drink at the after-concert party, and let that ghastly man talk me into bed. I felt so ashamed — so dirty — the next morning, but I didn't dare breathe a word of it to Greg. He's so jealous, he'd have flown right off the handle."

"It would appear, from his mood today that he knows about it now. Is that correct?" Falconer was getting there, but slower than he'd planned, due to Greg's sudden departure — he'd lost his advantage when that happened, and he hadn't been able to let off his bomb in a room that contained both of them.

"Perfectly correct. That filthy old pervert was dropping hints — Marcus, I mean — and I didn't know whether he was intending to tell Greg all about it, or use it to blackmail me back into his grubby little lair. I didn't know what else to do. He was obviously intent on making mischief, and the only thing I could think of doing was getting if off my chest, and trusting that everything would be all right.

"And I still don't know if it is. At first, Greg stormed out, and he stayed away longer than I'd expected. I was absolutely sure he'd left me for good, and that was it, as far as our marriage was concerned. Then he did come back. But apart from the few hours immediately after his return, he's been in a filthy mood ever since, and I don't know whether I'm relieved at his return, or not."

"Thank you, Mrs Markland. That was very brave of you, but I have to ask you some other questions, the answers to which are very important, and I want you, again, to be absolutely truthful with your answers," and he repeated the questions he had asked Delia Jephcott.

She just looked puzzled when confronted with the name "Jennifer Linden", and shook her head in answer. To the question of her being Summer's mother, her reaction was unexpectedly violent. She just stared at Falconer for a few seconds, her eyes full of hatred, then with a growl of, "Did that bastard Greg put you up to this?" she dissolved into tears, pouring her body into the cushioned embrace of an armchair, and covering her face with her arms to hide her misery and anger.

"Whatever have I said, Mrs Markland? I didn't mean to upset you like that." Falconer felt almost as devastated as *she* looked — at the swiftness of her disintegration; but there was a glimmer that he might be on to something here, and he wasn't going to let go of it.

Hoping that Carmichael would not go into "comfort-blanket" mode too quickly on this occasion, he asked again, "What have I said to upset you so?" This time he got an answer.

"I can't have children, you bloody fool! Who told you? *I-want-to know-who-told-you!*" she screeched, separating each word of the question, and thumping her hands on the arms of the chair in time to the words in her fury.

It was time Falconer backed off, and he did so immediately. "Nobody told me, Mrs Markland. I had no idea, I promise you." If this was acting on her part, it had the spark of genius in its sincerity; but he knew it wasn't, and he didn't hold out a lot of hope for the survival of their marriage. Gregory Markland may have returned to the marital home, but all the signs indicated that he wouldn't be staying there for long. Falconer had wandered, unknowingly, into a hornets' nest, and, now it was disturbed, he just wanted to get away from it.

"We'll be getting along then, Mrs Markland. Don't bother to show us out. We'll find our own way." Camilla was still glaring from her chair in absolute rage as they left.

VI

Squirrel Horsfall-Ertz was still an elderly bundle of misery when she opened her door to them. She walked

224

straight through the house, leading them to the back garden, where she stopped at a small, well-tended grave at the side, near the back door. "I like to have him near me," she informed them. "He was such a dear little thing, a joy to watch when he and his brother were play-fighting."

It was obvious that she was talking about her late dog, and that she still mourned its untimely end. Falconer had decided that, just for the sake of form, he ought to ask her a few questions to determine whether her grief might had been strong enough to turn to violence, when Bubble's murderer had moved into the same village as her, and apparently without a care in the world.

"Miss Horsfall-Ertz, I wonder if you would mind telling me where you were on Sunday night last?" he asked baldly, not wanting to beat around the bush and suffer any more outbursts of emotion. He'd had enough of those for one day. Although he knew it was only an illusion, his shoulders felt soaked with tears, and he'd seen enough of grief of one sort or another, for now.

"Last Sunday night — let me see — that was the day everyone did their party pieces over in the hall, wasn't it?"

"That's right, Miss Horsfall-Ertz, and the day after you threw a cup of hot tea over Mr Willoughby, not to mention brandishing a knife at him on Friday."

She blushed at the memories, but offered no defence, saying instead, "I was just so upset at having seen him, that I'm afraid I took to my bed. It seemed impossible and unfair that he was here in Stoney Cross,

225

and that I might run into him at any time on one of my little walks with Squeak. I couldn't bear the thought of that, and almost gave up the will to live. If it hadn't been for the kind vicar's visit, I doubt that I or Squeak would be here now.

"He gave me a stiff talking-to, pointed out that I might want to starve myself to death, but how was that fair to my little pet? Nothing was his fault, yet he'd been stuck in the house with no food, no water, and no attention. He said that, even if I didn't realise it, I was making the poor little darling suffer with me, and Squeak had no understanding of why it was happening. Well, that shook me out of my self-pity. Vicar talks a lot of sense, as well as his do-gooding. I'll always miss Bubble, but he made me realise that Squeak is still alive, and needs me to be well enough to look after him and love him. That certainly brought me to my senses, didn't it, my little darling?" she asked, looking adoringly at the small dog capering round her feet.

"So you didn't leave the house on Sunday evening, or during the night?" Falconer was now certain he was wasting his time, and even Carmichael must have been of the same mind, because he was putting away his notebook.

"I was in no fit state to do anything on Sunday night, Inspector. I suppose you could say that, for a while, I was a broken woman. His face just brought it all back so vividly, that that was all I could think about. Well, least said, soonest mended," she concluded, and looked up at him.

226

"Thank you very much for your time. We'll be off now, and leave you in peace." There was nothing here for them.

VII

Consulting his watch, Falconer realised that it was a quarter to five, and the members of the search party would no doubt be making their way back to The Inn on the Green, if they were not already gathered there. "I think we'll wait for Miss Wingfield-Heyes to come to us, Carmichael. We can catch her tomorrow, when she comes in to the station to make a formal statement. She might have heard or seen a car; although living in the opposite direction to Ms Palister, I have my doubts. Still, we'd better ask, for form's sake."

"Good idea, sir. It'd be a shame to miss a vital clue just because of a spot of laziness on the interviewing front," Carmichael mumbled, and Falconer, sort of hearing him, decided not to ask him to repeat his opinion. If what he'd heard was correct, then Carmichael was right, but if he repeated it more loudly, it may do something indefinable to their relationship, and he didn't want that to happen. He had a feeling they were working their way towards a successful partnership, weird though his acting sergeant could be at times. He had never expected to think such a thing, but he had a feeling they were bonding into a good team, each with his own strengths to add to the whole.

Arriving back at the pub car park, he saw the gathering of bodies, all of them in uniform. They must have been back for some time, he surmised, if all the civilians had been dismissed. But this proved not to be so, for when they all entered The Inn for a debrief, there were three villagers already in the bar, nursing pint glasses. The uniforms had bidden the two detectives to enter, as they had something to show for their search, and PC Green, as the longest-serving officer, had adopted the role of spokesperson.

After a generous offer of coffee — on the house — had been made and accepted, and the "*Closed*" sign was displayed at the entrances lest anyone from the village have an early thirst and try to gain entrance, everyone settled down so that the constable could update the plain-clothes on their finds. Before Falconer cleared his throat to indicate that silence was required, there had been a quiet hum of excited conversation, people speculating on what exactly today's finds would mean.

"Come on then, what have you got for me? Anything useful? I can see you've had a result, from your faces." Falconer smiled as he asked this, turning towards the constable for his contribution.

"We did find a couple of things, sir, but I don't know as how they'd be pertinent to the disappearance. It seems we may have come across a couple of items more suited to being involved in your murder enquiry."

This made both Falconer and Carmichael prick up their ears. "Well, go on, man! Don't keep us in suspense!"

"It was the group that went to the north-west that found them, sir. They were in a clump of brambles on the boundary of the sports ground, not far from the rear of Mr Willoughby's property."

"They? They? Come on, man, what are *they*?"

"We've got a club hammer and a fragment of fine material of a knitted nature, charred around the edges, as if someone had attempted to burn it. Lucky for us, in retrospect, that the foggy conditions made it so damp that night, and that there were brambles there to catch a-hold of it. Any use to you, sir?" This concluding question was asked with a smug smile slapped right across PC Green's chops.

"My God, Constable, you've only gone and found the murder weapon, and evidence of the other silk stocking! Where are they?"

"All dealt with, sir. Positions marked, items photographed, bagged, and taken away by Scene-of-Crime chaps."

"Why didn't you phone me?"

"There might've been more to find. We just got the chaps in to do their job, and carried on searching. At that point, we were only half an hour into the search, and didn't feel we could give up that easily. There might've been something to find that was pertinent to the abduction — disappearance — whatever you want to call it."

"Good man! There should be an appeal out on the local radio at six, and the *Gazette* is primed and ready to go at a word from me, if need be. If this gets much beyond tomorrow, we're probably looking for a body, rather than some sort of hostage. Now, which of your grand officers found these objects?"

"Twinkle, sir — that is, WPC Starr. Step forward, young lady, and take a bow."

A figure detached itself from the scrum of uniformed bodies. WPC Starr was of slight build, her short dark hair slicked back from her face like a cap. She looked more like an elf in fancy dress than a serving police officer, but she had proved her worth today. Taking a low stage-bow to left and right, she sat down again, a little flustered at this un-sought notoriety, to a scattering of applause from her colleagues. The inspector hardly noticed as he rose from his seat, so excited was he by the finds.

"OK!" Falconer reclaimed their attention by holding his hand in the air for silence. "Although you've had a great result for the murder, we have to get on with looking for this missing girl. I want you to start house-to-house enquiries in the village. Knock at every door and ask if anyone saw anything at all of Summer Leighton after she left The Inn yesterday morning. If we get no results from that, we're going to have to search every property, inside and out, tomorrow. Have a look in sheds and garages today, if you can. You never know what you're going to find.

"And remember, I mean every house — that is, with the exception of (here, he cleared his throat in an embarrassed manner) Blackbird Cottage in Stoney Cross Lane. I'm going there myself now, in pursuit of information in connection with the Willoughby case, and I can have a scout around and ask a few questions while I'm about it." He was blushing to the roots of his hair as he bade them get on with the job, embarrassed by his hidden agenda, and positive that everyone could see through his motives and look right into his heart.

When he and Carmichael were alone in The Inn, the three villagers having decided that the excitement was over for the day, and that they needed to be elsewhere to boast of their exploits with the search party, Falconer phoned David Porter of the *Gazette* again to report that there was still no news, and to check that he was prepared to put a piece in the paper tomorrow, in case the house-to-house enquiries turned up nothing.

David Porter, however, had news of his own to impart. "You know you were asking me about Marcus Willoughby?" he asked, not realising what an impact the information he was about to offer would have. "I've known him since schooldays; we are — we *were* — of an age. Did you have any idea that he didn't used to be called Marcus Willoughby — that that was a pseudonym only?"

Falconer nearly dropped the phone. "What?"

"That's right. He was a right arsy little bastard at school, full of cheek, and boy, could he hold a grudge. Universally disliked would be about right. I only gave him a job 'for the sake of auld lang syne', and, as I told you, I've lived to regret my nostalgic generosity, for he was nothing but trouble, even after all these years."

"What was he known as at school?" Falconer took a chance. "It wouldn't perhaps be Norman Clegg, would it?"

"Now, how the *hell* did you know that? And don't say it was just a shot in the dark, because that's impossible." Porter had had his thunder well and truly stolen, but had realised, at once, that this must have some bearing on the man's demise.

"I can't tell you at the moment. It's privileged information, but be assured that you'll be the first to know, when I'm able to disclose it."

"I'd better be, Falconer. I'd better be. Oh, and by the way, I've spoken to the local radio johnnies, and they're going to put a bit into the news tonight — asking the missing girl, or anyone with information on her whereabouts, to come forward, etc., etc."

Offering his thanks for Porter's efforts with local radio, and promising to ring again later, to confirm that he definitely needed the newspaper article, he ended the call, and marched purposefully towards the car, not daring to look Carmichael in the face, for fear of what he would see there.

VIII

The short drive from The Inn to Blackbird Cottage was undertaken in absolute silence. Falconer dared not speak, from embarrassment that Carmichael had realised his intentions in making this visit at all, considering Serena had had nothing to do with the Festival. Carmichael was quiet because he had discovered a chink in his superior's normally impregnable armour, and was diplomatic enough not to cause him any further embarrassment by bringing up the subject.

(There definitely *was* more to Carmichael than met the eye — an opinion that Falconer had formed earlier in their relationship, and was now in the process of confirming, after his acting sergeant's behaviour during interviews with traumatised ladies.)

There was no car in the drive as they drew up outside the cottage, and that was a huge disappointment to the inspector. It looked like he'd got himself all hyped up to speak to Serena, only to find out that she wasn't there. Taking no chances, however, Falconer rang the doorbell and had his way with the knocker, while Carmichael went round to the back, to make sure she wasn't in the garden, the car just having gone for a service, or something prosaic like that.

She wasn't, and it hadn't, or didn't appear to have. There was no window in the small garage, so there was no way of telling whether she had just put her car away, as she had felt unable to drive it safely with her injured ankle, or actually gone out. Squinting through the windows bore no fruit either. The cottage was locked up, all the windows closed, and with the look that all houses have when their inhabitants are not there — inscrutable and secret. "Maybe a friend called round — on foot, I mean — and took her for a drive, sir? Perhaps she needed some shopping, and her friend took her into Carsfold to do it?"

Carmichael was doing his best to relieve the anxious expression on his superior's face, but his suggestions didn't seem to be helping much. "Sorry, Carmichael. What with a murder and a disappearance on our plates, I can't help feeling pessimistic today, and visualising the worst possible scenario. Don't worry — it'll pass. Let's go round the back together and have a good look, at least do what we would have expected a uniform to do. We can always come back tomorrow, have a look inside, and ask her if she saw anything of Miss Leighton."

"And at least we know who Norman Clegg is — or rather, was, so that's one mystery cleared up, sir," Carmichael offered, in an attempt to steer Falconer towards counting his blessings and not his curses.

"You're right, but that doesn't get us any further forward with finding out who Jennifer Linden is, does it?" Falconer was resisting his colleague's efforts, and was in danger of falling into a sulk, like a child deprived of an expected treat.

"And we've got the murder weapon now." Carmichael wasn't giving up without a fight.

"I know, but I'd put my shirt on it having been wiped clean of any prints." Come to think of it, he'd like to put Carmichael's shirt on something, too — preferably a bonfire! "Come on, I'll drop you back at the station so you can collect your car. I've had enough for one day, and I'm sure you're eager to get yourself ready for your visit to your lady love."

"Don't forget the kids, sir. They're just as important to me. As far as I'm concerned, they come as a package, and I wouldn't want it any other way."

Just for a moment — a very short moment — Falconer felt very jealous.

CHAPTER
SIXTEEN

Monday, 14th September

I

Monday morning found Falconer late into the office, and Carmichael was already at his desk hard at it, when he arrived. "Morning, sir. Get lost on the way in?" the acting sergeant offered jovially. He'd obviously had a good night. Falconer had *not* had that advantage. He had been haunted by nightmares of Serena, dead, kidnapped or in danger, and he had woken every hour or so, in a cold sweat, relieved to find it was only a dream, not a reality.

"Good morning, Carmichael. No need to ask how your evening went."

"Reports are all typed up and on your desk, from the house-to-house yesterday."

"Anything in them?"

"I don't know, sir. They were addressed to you, so I didn't look at them."

Was there anyone so honest (or so uncurious) in the whole of the constabulary as this man?

Falconer reached for his phone, checking a number in a file in his desk, and began to make enquiries about

Marcus Willoughby's telephone account. He had taken a while to clear his mind when he had got home the previous evening, and had realised that this information may be very useful to them.

They now knew who Norman Clegg was, but they had yet to find Jennifer Linden. Not only had she known Marcus Willoughby (Falconer could not bring himself to use any other name, so used had he got to using this one), and known him intimately, but she was also the mother of the missing girl. She might have information that would be vital to both cases. She might even have Summer Leighton staying with her — this whole second case could be that innocent.

If Summer had meant she was going to see her mother when she called out as she left The Inn, they could be sitting together now, drinking tea, none the wiser about all the kerfuffle the younger woman's absence was causing. There was no guarantee, after all, that the mother actually lived in the area. Summer might have left without her car, because she was being given a lift. She could have been picked up from Stoney Cross, and be anywhere by now.

So far, her disappearance had only been broadcast on local radio stations, and should be in the local paper today. If she wasn't found before this evening, however, news of her disappearance would be, not only on the local television news, but on the national news as well. If she still hadn't turned up, there was at least a possibility that this would tip

Summer the wink that she ought to announce her whereabouts.

And, if that didn't get any response from the missing girl, it would probably bring people who knew her out of the woodwork, and they could find out where she lived. She had taken her handbag with her, and Peregrine had failed to take any details, so they didn't even know her address, yet. Why couldn't she just have written it in her diary, like everyone else did? The worst-case scenario was that they found her dead, and he did not relish the added complication of a second murder investigation.

Marcus's itemised telephone bill would at least show them the numbers he had called, and one of them might have been Summer's mother. He had no idea on what terms they had parted, or why she had put up their daughter for adoption in the first place, and he saw no point in wasting time on guesswork. And if that didn't produce results, it might get them on to somebody who had known Marcus at the time Summer was born — someone who might know more about the prevailing circumstances than he did, at the moment.

His reverie was interrupted by an internal call from the inevitable Bob Bryant, to say that there was a young lady to see him, and that he had put her in an interview room.

"What name did she give, Bob?"

"Bit of a mouthful, sir. She said she was Miss Araminta Wingfield-Heyes — mean anything to you?"

"Sure does! Thanks Bob, I'm on my way." This was a bit of luck, her coming into the station so promptly — it was only just gone nine. He could get his few questions for her out of the way, and be able to give his complete attention to how to move the cases on.

II

He found Minty sitting in the dingy room, playing with a plastic cup of (plastic) tea, and reading the graffiti carved into or written on the table in front of her, her head turned to one side so that she could decipher one of the comments which was at an awkward angle. Her face, when she turned it towards him, was smiling, and just a little bit excited. "I think I've remembered something, Inspector, but I don't know if it means anything." Where had he heard that before?!

"Try me, and we'll see." This was music to Falconer's ears. The quicker he could get things wrapped up, the quicker he could arrange to take Serena out. If he could tidy the murder away, and Summer's disappearance went bigger, maybe even with a ransom note (but to whom, he could not imagine, knowing so little about her), it would probably be handed to someone of a higher rank, and he would be free to do what he wanted for a while, God willing. He didn't even want to consider how much time he would be tied up for, if her body was found.

Minty tried him. "I was talking to Sadie yesterday after you'd been to see her, and she told me about the car she'd seen."

"Yes, go on," Falconer prompted, as she'd paused momentarily.

"It's just that I'm sure and certain that I heard a car as well, just as I was getting back to my own house, after — you know what."

"And you reckoned that was about one-thirty a.m., if my memory serves me correctly." Falconer was excited too, now. The information she was about to give him might be crucial — and he damned well hoped it *would* be — so much depended on it, including his future happiness. Let the case end! He'd had enough of it!

"That's right — when I got in — about then. The funny thing was, even though I heard it coming in my direction — it sounded as if it was in a very low gear. Because of the fog, I suppose — it never actually passed me."

So those two drunken women, both bent on doing Willoughby a bad turn, had been sneaking around in the dark, one after the other, and so close together in time, that they had both heard the arrival of the murderer's car? Falconer wondered if they'd worked it out yet, and if they hadn't, how they'd feel when they did. A few minutes later for either of them, and they might not have been here to tell the tale. It really was a wonder they hadn't blundered into each other in the dark, and scared the living daylights out of one another.

239

Realising that he had been distracted by these thoughts, he continued, "And it was definitely coming from the direction of the High Street?"

"Oh yes, I'd stake my great-grandmother's life on it," she claimed, with a little twinkle at him, to reassure him that she was only having her little joke.

"So, it never passed you? It couldn't have been far enough down the High Street to, perhaps, have turned down School Lane, could it?"

"Absolutely not! The engine was definitely turned off. The noise just stopped, before it got to me. I'd even staggered right to the edge of the hedge and stopped — you know the pavement ends after The Old Barn, and doesn't go as far as my place?"

"Now you come to mention it, I do remember. So, this car might have been driven on to Mr Willoughby's property?"

"That's the only thing I can think of." Minty's eyes were still glowing with excitement, at remembering something important. "And there was something else, too."

"What?" What else could there possibly be, at one-thirty a.m. on a foggy night?

"The exhaust! It was just starting to go, sounded as if it had just blown a little hole in the pipe."

"Are you sure?"

"My Uncle Bob owns several garages now, but when I was young, he only had the one, not having had the chance to grow the business, and I used to spend hours watching him work on cars. I can tell you just about anything that's wrong with any part of a car, just by hearing it running."

What a stroke of luck! Now, all they had to do was to find a local car with a hole in its exhaust, tie it up with a motive, and Bob's your uncle — or in this case, Minty's uncle! Yet, this was a little short-sighted of him, he realised, for the murderer could still be someone with an older axe to grind than was to be found in Stoney Cross, but he could hope, couldn't he?

Falconer was grinning when he showed Minty out of the police station. He had nearly shaken the hand off her, and just resisted the urge to hug her. He was returning now to his office, to give the good news to Carmichael. He'd have to speak to Ms Palister again, to see if she remembered a slightly blown exhaust, but he could do that later, when he went back to Stoney Cross to see Serena.

He quailed at the thought of needing to speak to Sadie again. She was quite an overpowering young woman. Young men, he knew how to deal with from his Army days, but women, young or not so young, were still a mystery to him — one which he was hoping to solve in the not-too-distant future, and this thought cheered him considerably.

He entered the office whistling, an occurrence unique in Carmichael's experience of the inspector, and it brought his head up with a jerk, to witness this previously unheard-of phenomenon.

III

The rest of the morning passed in a flurry of paperwork, as did the most part of the afternoon, checking through the reports from the search team, geeing-up Forensics about the presence (or not) of fingerprints or DNA on the club hammer and fragment of stocking, and going through the results of the house-to-house enquiry from the previous day.

At four o'clock, when Falconer was just tidying away his desk for departure, having warned Carmichael that they would be making yet another trip to Stoney Cross to visit Blackbird Cottage, his internal phone rang, and he found himself summoned to Superintendent "Jelly' Chivers" office for an update, and it wasn't until five o'clock that they were free to leave.

The cottage was as they had left it yesterday — still no answer to their summons on the doorbell and knocker, the car still not on the drive. A quick peer through the windows provided no answers, and an attempt by Falconer to see if the phone might be picked up, Serena perhaps being merely out of their sight-line, was also unsuccessful. He had never had a mobile number for her, so they were completely snookered for now.

The time of day had encouraged Falconer to urge Carmichael to take his own car. That way he, at least, would not have to return to the office and, at the moment, the inspector certainly had nothing better to do than to go back to see if there had been any progress made in his (relatively short) absence.

Carmichael, it seemed, had nothing better on either, and so it was that they re-entered the office to find an envelope on Falconer's desk, containing an itemised telephone bill for Willoughby's three short days'

242

residence in The Old Barn. There weren't that many calls listed, maybe a couple of dozen or so, but one of them hit Falconer straight between the eyes.

Serena's number was staring up at him, called twice within that time. But she'd said she had never met him before. What was going on? He had to find out! It wasn't right that the house was empty, her ankle being in the condition it was. He needed to get back out there, to see that nothing had happened to her. How had Willoughby known her?

Wait a minute, she had said something along the lines of "I've never met anyone called Marcus Willoughby". That was an ambiguous remark, in the light of the knowledge they now had, that Willoughby had spent part of his life as Norman Clegg. What if she had known him as Norman Clegg? What if saying she had never known anyone of "that name" was her being economical with the truth, telling only one part of the story? What if he had some sort of hold over her? What if she'd done something stupid? Or even just fallen down the stairs? Falconer knew that most of these questions were ridiculous, and just the result of panic, but his mind was whirling. He couldn't help himself and called for Carmichael to join him on the return trip to her house.

Carmichael, however, seemed to ignore his urgent summons, apparently lost in his own thoughts. He was, in fact, still gnawing at whatever it was at the back of his mind — the something that wasn't quite right, which didn't add up — and he'd nearly had it then, when he finally became aware of the inspector's repeated summons for him to leave the station.

IV

At the same time that Harry Falconer was going out of his mind with worry, Adella Ravenscastle was approaching Squirrel Horsfall-Ertz's house, having just returned from a very important trip to Market Darley, and with a strange, quivering lump under the front of her cardigan.

Squirrel opened her front door and noticed the movement as she greeted her visitor, a puzzled look bunching the lines and wrinkles of her elderly face. "What on earth have you got there?" she asked, her words coinciding with a little whine and a "wuff" from the now squirming cardigan front. Lifting a Yorkshire terrier puppy from beneath its woolly covering, Adella handed it over to Squirrel, a look of triumph on her face.

"Wherever did you get him," Squirrel beamed, a glint of joy, and also of hope, in her eyes.

"He's for you, dear Squirrel."

"I couldn't possibly accept him," she said, but her look of longing told a different story. "They're so terribly expensive. It's just too much," she cooed, as she cradled the little dog lovingly in her arms.

"Absolute rot, Squirrel! I couldn't bear to see you suffering any more, so I went down to Carsfold in the early hours of Monday morning . . ."

"You never?"

"I most certainly did. And I dropped a note through the door for Mrs Outen — you know, that old lady that breeds Yorkies?"

"But I can't accept him! Because of the cost, you know."

"It's not a matter of the cost," said Adella, smiling at the adoration and covetousness in the old woman's eyes.

"Then I'll pay you back — every penny — if you'll give me time."

"There's absolutely no need, for he didn't cost me a penny. I left a note explaining that I was in urgent need of a puppy, then I telephoned her the next day. She said she had what she called 'a runt' left over from her last litter, that she'd be happy for you to have."

"Oh, how kind of her, and of you as well, of course. I don't know how to thank you, but you make sure you pass on my thanks to her. No one could have given me a better present, and she must have looked after him well, because he doesn't look a bit like a runt to me."

"I'll pass your thanks on, and don't think anything of it. Just give him a name, introduce him to Squeak, and enjoy him."

"Oh, I will, Mrs Ravenscastle! I will, believe you me!"

On her way back to The Vicarage, Adella was aware of a good deed shining in a murky world. She just wondered how she was going to explain to Benedict that her gift hadn't exactly been free — had, in fact, been rather expensive, and that they'd probably have to tighten their belts till Christmas. But she knew her husband, and he would probably just be delighted that Squirrel was no longer living in misery, and was having her life invigorated by the energy of a new puppy.

V

What with one thing and another, the afternoon had completely disappeared now, and lights were going on in shops, houses and streets. It was a dull day, and the weather, remembering that it should be getting into its autumn attire, had donned a cloak of iron grey that promised rain sometime during the evening, and the daylight had leeched away unusually early, cowed into submission.

Carmichael, in his own car now, had trouble keeping up with the pace that Falconer set, so worried was the inspector about Serena. Falconer was already out of his car and hammering on the door as his colleague drew to a halt behind the Boxster. There were no lights on in the house. This could just mean that Serena had gone away for a few days, but everyone who had been interviewed had been asked not to leave the area if possible and, at least, let the police know if they couldn't avoid doing so. There had been no call logged from Blackbird Cottage which, given Falconer's frame of mind, could only hint at something sinister.

He was frantic now, calling Carmichael to come round to the back of the house with him, where he picked up a heavy stone, one of many that lined a flower border. Hefting it in his hand to check its weight,

246

he took a firm grip and broke a pane of glass in the back door. Carefully clearing away the biggest spikes of glass, he put his hand through the hole and turned the key before Carmichael could finish asking him what the hell he thought he was doing.

VI

Inside, the house was airless and still, the only sound that of the mewing of cats. Looking down, Falconer became aware that the animals' food bowls were empty, as were their water bowls, and that he had two furry creatures weaving their way between his legs, calling for succour. Carmichael, softhearted as he was, began immediately to search the cupboards for cat food, replenishing their water bowls first, knowing that lack of fluid could be much more harmful than lack of food. His face was still a perplexed mask.

Falconer, on the other hand, had raced into the living room, stopping to look behind the door and round the back of the sofa, before heading towards the stairs, taking them two at a time, so desperate was he to find either Serena, or some clue to her whereabouts. There was no one in the bathroom, the master bedroom, or the airing cupboard. What a state I must be in, to have looked in there, he thought. The last door he approached was that of the spare room.

Opening the door to this last-chance saloon, the curtains of which were drawn together, he heard a slight moan, and caught sight of a figure in the single bed. "Serena!" he yelled, rushing forward. At the same moment as he had called her name, Carmichael had shouted from the kitchen.

"Ankle, sir! Got it!" he yelled, and similarly headed for the stairs, taking them *three* at a time (well, he *was* a big lad!)

He found Falconer staring at the figure on the bed, covered with a sheet. Having recovered his wits with his memory, he lifted a hand to flick on the light, as his superior officer kept muttering, "Not her! Not her! Where is she? What am I going to do?" Falconer was just standing there, talking quietly but desperately to himself. "It's not Serena, Carmichael! What am I going to do? Where is she? I need to know!"

Carmichael led him gently to a basket-weave chair and sat him down. The figure on the bed was not, indeed, Serena, but then Carmichael had known it wouldn't be. The detail that had eluded him for so long had been to do with on which ankle Ms Lyddiard actually wore her bandage. Finding it carelessly stuffed into the cupboard where the cat food was kept had been enough of a catalyst to produce the answer: both! When he thought back, it seemed to move from leg to leg, almost with a life of its own, and nobody had really noticed, being too caught up with their own lives and problems.

Dragging his attention back to the figure under the sheet, he noticed for the first time that a gastro-nasal tube had been inserted, as had a fluid drip in the arm. A catheter bag drooped below the sheet, nearly full.

"Call an ambulance, please," croaked a broken voice from the corner of the room, and Carmichael took his mobile out of his pocket to fulfil this quiet request from his still-caring but heartbroken superior.

Carmichael, forward-thinking and insightful, also made a call for a SOCO team, and a uniform to collect two cat baskets from the station's contact in the RSPCA. The uniformed officer could then hold the fort while he, Carmichael, took the inspector home, before returning to Blackbird Cottage to wind up the day's proceedings. He had realised Falconer's feelings for Serena, and thought he knew how he must be feeling. His current logic was, if Kerry and the kids came as a package so, then, did Serena and her two cats. He would take them in his car with the boss, as a sort of solace.

After the short, silent drive Carmichael guided Falconer into his house and gently let him down into an armchair. He then made a pot of tea, placed the biscuit barrel on the tray, and carried the lot through to the sitting room, even going so far as to pour the amber liquid, and hand it to the inspector, who took it in a dazed manner. Falconer just sat holding it, staring at the cup and saucer as if he had no idea what they were, and was trying to find some rational explanation for why he had them in his hand.

Carmichael then fetched the cat baskets, placed them gently on the floor and opened their doors. Mycroft would have to make of it what he would. He could like it or lump it, although it would be the inspector's final say, as to whether they stayed, or whether they were too painful a reminder of their previous owner. He'd put his money on the former, though, knowing how fond Falconer was of cats.

Before he left, he went through to the kitchen, set the cat flap to "in only", and filled up the bowls already on the floor, getting extra ones out of a cupboard so that there was plenty of everything for all three animals. That might not prevent all of the "getting to know you" fighting, there being no need to share a bowl for that, but it would certainly help towards discouraging it. The extra "ado" that this new admixture would create in the household should act as a distraction for Falconer. If he was forever having to make sure every cat got on with the other two, he would not be thinking about what he believed he had lost.

Healing would take a long time and, promising to return when he had finished in Stoney Cross, to make his boss an omelette, Carmichael set off, once more, for the house in Stoney Stile Lane, wondering what on earth Summer had been doing in that bed, hooked up to drips and a catheter, and seemingly unconscious.

VII

Back in Blackbird Cottage, he found the ambulance already departed, the SOCO team just finishing up. "Find anything to enlighten us?" he asked, seeming, as it were, to have deserted the ship, just when it was getting underway.

"We found a spare set of keys in a kitchen drawer, took a look in the garage, in case there were any more undiscovered bodies. The car was still there, and it's been confirmed that the exhaust was blowing. She'd tried to make some sort of repair with what appears to be the plaster they do your limbs up with — can't remember the name for the moment — but it wouldn't have been much good. Paris! That's it!

"We also found some ampoules of heavy-duty sedative in the bathroom cupboard — the sort you put into the bags of saline drips. And there were several more saline bags in the main bedroom. She'd got that poor girl knocked out in a proper little hospital set-up. I've got absolutely no idea at all what was going on. Have you?"

"Sort of — I'm not sure." Carmichael was working on it.

"Oh, and before I forget, there was an envelope fell out from between the pillows when the paramedics moved her. It's addressed to Inspector Falconer. Here it is," and the officer handed over a white envelope, thickly padded by its contents. "Better see he gets to have a look at it, before we have to book it in as evidence. It may not shed any light on this little mystery but, if it does, we're going to need it."

Carmichael carefully tucked the envelope away in his pocket, saw the remaining police personnel off the premises and made sure that everything was switched off and locked up. As he unlocked his car, he looked back at the cottage, sitting innocently in its pretty chrysanthemum halo, and, as he drove away to deliver Serena's last message to the inspector, he thought, if only walls could talk!

VIII

Carmichael had been as good as his word, and had returned to Falconer's house, given him the envelope, and made a fresh pot of tea and an omelette. The inspector had spurned the tea, pouring himself, instead, a very large glass of red wine. He did, however, consent to sit at the table in the kitchen and pick at the omelette, which was surprisingly good, despite his lack of appetite.

By the time he had picked the last fragment from the plate, he had poured himself a third glass of wine, knowing that there were no answers to be found in the bottom of a glass, but not particularly caring. What a difference a day makes — wasn't there a song that went like that? He couldn't believe the high spirits he had felt only that morning, which already seemed a lifetime ago. He couldn't believe the hopes he had held, the promise for the future; even, maybe, for the rest of his life. Now, here he was, in hell, his dreams shattered into as many pieces as the pane of glass in Serena's back door, the future yawning before him, empty — a lonely void. He'd never experienced loneliness before, and was just making its acquaintance.

Although Carmichael had thoughtfully cleared the plate and washed up before he had left, Falconer was still sitting at the kitchen table, swallowing mouthfuls of wine rather than sipping it, the nearly-empty bottle on the table, waiting to be drained. He took another swig, and put his hand into his pocket to remove the fat envelope that Carmichael had handed him on arrival. He sat for a while in silence, just looking at the handwriting, the tidy calligraphy that joined the letters of his name, and judged them as beautiful as the woman who had written them.

Finally, he put the envelope down on the table, fetched himself another bottle of wine, filled his glass with the last of the first bottle, and sat down again. The time had come.

Picking up the envelope and inserting his thumb beneath the flap, he had time to notice how every little move he made appeared to be in slow motion. Time was indeed elastic, but whether this was due to the wine he had imbibed, the fierce emotions he was feeling torn apart by, or a combination of the two, he had no idea, nor did he care. This was it! Like Pandora, he was opening the box, and letting out all the sins of the world. At that particular moment he had forgotten what had been left in the box afterwards — hope — but he neither thought about this, nor cared. All he could think about was the empty box.

There were several sheets of paper, covered on both sides in tiny but immaculate writing. Leaning his elbows on the table, he began to read, his eyes moving slowly, not wanting to miss a single word, phrase or nuance.

My dear Harry, *he read,*

By the time you get this letter, I shall be either in prison, or gone, but I needed to let you know how I feel about you, before I disappeared completely from your life. I know I have a lot of explaining to do, but I shall come to that in the pages that follow. For now, I just want to write down how deeply I have felt for you since the moment we met.

I have never felt an attraction like that before and, if you will forgive me for being so forward, I think you felt the same. I also think, given normal circumstances, that we would have made a great couple. It may even have been that we were able to have a child — I'm not quite too old yet! But it was not to be. I realise that we will never see each other again, and it breaks my heart!

Please don't look for me, my darling, for I'm very good at living a nomadic life, and have done so since my youth. Stoney Cross was my first attempt to settle down since I gave birth to my daughter — many, many years ago.

Yes, you will have already realised that the young woman known as Summer Leighton is the result of a foolish infatuation from which I suffered while still a teenager. That man was so much older than me, but then, when does one ever listen to one's parents? I certainly didn't, but I also found myself unable to cope with the thought of an abortion. In my eyes then, as it still is now, abortion is murder. No one who doesn't want to be pregnant in this day and age needs to be so. I was careless. I made a stupid mistake which I have been paying for ever since.

I had the child, and handed it straight over for adoption, not wanting to hold it, to look at it, or to take any risk of forming a bond with it. Marcus —

he was plain old Norman Clegg in those days, and I was young Jenny Linden — didn't seem much taken with the idea of fatherhood at the time, either, so this seemed to be the easiest way to draw a line under the whole sorry experience.

Anyway, to cut a long story short, Summer — for that is how I must now refer to her — had decided to trace her birth parents. I had changed my name before she came of age, to make myself harder to find, not realising that her father had also changed his, for reasons of vanity.

He telephoned me, you know, twice — to let me know our daughter had finally caught up with us. He, an elderly man by now, seemed to revel in the fact that he had a pretty daughter he could hang on his arm for decoration, but he knew how I would feel about it.

I nearly screamed when I saw him in the village hall, and pretended to sprain my ankle. (You must have guessed that I was rather careless about the bandage, but I didn't think anyone else would notice. People are usually so caught up in themselves, so subsumed by their own ego, that they don't notice little details about others, so I didn't think too much of it.)

But the thought that I might bump into him at any time made me determined to move on. Then, when he told me that our daughter had been to see him, and "verified her credentials" as it were, I knew I had to do something about him before I left. The whole idea of having borne his child had grown to nightmare proportions. It was never anything to do with Summer as a person.

Anyway, it was I who killed him, disposing of the weapons in the scrub at the edge of the field behind his house. It was I who forwarded his broadcast to the radio station, in a fit of spite, for what he had done to the young girl (me) who was full of hope. I'd done some work in a hospital, and used to do a little bit for the hospital radio with short stories — recording them at home, then sending them in. I thought that, with everyone thinking I was incapacitated, no one would connect me with the murder — that I had a perfect alibi. But I hadn't taken into account my daughter's tenacity.

It was also I, as you will have realised, who left poor Summer in the state in which you have obviously found her. There was nothing else I could do. I'd hoped that her father had not had the opportunity to identify me, but I was wrong. Then I hoped that he had not passed on where I was to her, and I was wrong about that too.

When she turned up on my doorstep, I was stunned and repulsed at the same time — please don't judge me for this, for she had her father in her eyes. I asked her in, of course, and made her a cup of tea, having made some excuse to go upstairs — actually to find some sleeping tablets to dissolve in her cup. When she passed out, I carried her upstairs — she was only a little thing, and I'm very wiry, having been involved in dancing and nursing which are both physically demanding jobs. I knew then that it was time to run, for I could not escape justice with her around. Discovery would have been inevitable, and I just couldn't face it.

I couldn't, of course, kill her, for she was the innocent in all this. I just wish she'd delayed her visit and given me a day or two more to make my arrangements to leave. But she didn't, and you know, now, how I dealt with that. I also put a letter in the post as I left the village, to the local police station, duplicating this confession, for the sake of the girl. She deserves some explanation.

I wish I had known you when I was Jenny Linden. But I stopped being her the moment that man impregnated me, and ruined all the plans I had for the rest of my life. I've mourned Jenny's passing for many years now, but she died at Summer's conception, and I was condemned to a life without roots.

That's about it, then, Harry, except to ask you if you could find it in your heart to take on my darling little Ruby, and old naughty paws, Tar Baby. They need you now.

I shall always love you, and I mourn what might have been.

And don't ever try to find me, for I shall be far, far away, and very well hidden.

Goodbye,

with all my love,

Serena xxxxxxx.

Harry Falconer let the thin sheets of paper slip from his fingers, dropped his head on to his arms, and wept.

Other titles published by Ulverscroft:

TIGHTROPE

Andrea Frazer

After entering a house where a commotion has been overheard, two community police officers make a horrific discovery. Detective Inspector Olivia Hardy and Detective Sergeant Lauren Groves are dispatched to investigate, triggering a major case that ends up with Hardy being usurped as the Senior Investigating Officer. It's yet another problem for Hardy, as she already suspects that husband Hal is having an affair. Meanwhile, as Groves descends into alcoholism after her husband's desertion, both officers' lives seem to be spiralling out of control. When a baby's body is found at the back of the police station, Hardy takes the unpleasant case, determined to succeed and show the world she's still capable — but things don't turn out exactly as planned . . .

A NECESSARY MURDER

M. J. Tjia

Stoke Newington, 1863: Little Margaret Lovejoy is found brutally murdered in the outhouse at her family's estate. A few days later, a man is cut down in a similar manner on the doorstep of courtesan and professional detective Heloise Chancey's prestigious address. Meanwhile, her maid, Amah Li Leen, must confront events from her past that appear to have erupted into the present day. Once again, Heloise is caught up in a maelstrom of murder and deceit that threatens to reach into the very heart of her existence.